# Tricksters from Fables & Mythology

**Anitha Murthy** is a software consultant by profession. She also loves to write and dabbles in many genres, both online and in print. Her short stories have been featured in various anthologies, her books have been published by Talking Cub (an imprint of Speaking Tiger), and picture books have been published by Pratham.

# Tricksters from Fables & Mythology

## Timeless Trickster Tales Retold

Anitha Murthy

RUPA

Published by
Rupa Publications India Pvt. Ltd 2025
161-B/4, Gulmohar House,
Yusuf Sarai Community Centre,
New Delhi 110049

*Sales centres:*
Bengaluru Chennai
Hyderabad Kolkata Mumbai



This is a work of fiction. Names, characters, places and incidents are either the product of the author's imagination or are used fictitiously and any resemblance to any actual person, living or dead, events or locales is entirely coincidental.



P-ISBN: 978-93-7003-063-3
E-ISBN: 978-93-7003-682-6

First impression 2025

10 9 8 7 6 5 4 3 2 1



Printed in India

*To Lalitha, my mother,*
*the most resourceful person I've ever known*

# Contents

# Preface

Every culture has its own set of myths, legends and fables.

There are many commonalities across these stories. For example, every culture has a creation myth that describes the beginning of the world—some say, for instance, that the world came into being from an egg, others, that it just appeared out of chaos.

Similarly, there are many stories about heroes who go on adventures and achieve greatness. Sometimes, this greatness is achieved through sheer bravery and courage; at other times, victory is achieved through some sort of trickery or deceit. Every culture has its unique set of tricksters who go around causing trouble, while also resolving tricky or even dangerous problems with their intelligence and wit. In India itself, we have a rich tradition of stories about these wise troublemakers, right from Narada of the gods, to Birbal and Tenali Rama.

This book presents a selection of such trickster tales from all over the world. Some are familiar figures; others are not so familiar. Some of the stories can be quite grisly, although an attempt has been made to keep them fairly sanitized. Some minor liberties have been taken with the stories to make for more interesting reading, for after all, this is a retelling of stories that have been handed down through the ages, each narrator adding his or her own twist and dash of spice. A couple of stories have been excerpted from longer tales, since it would be futile to pack every little detail and plot twist into such a collection of short stories. It is hoped that the reader will enjoy this assortment of tales, and will devour it as a delicious treat of tricks.

# Trouble in Paradise

*In Hindu mythology, Narada is a well-known figure. Depicted as a travelling, musically-inclined sage with a set of wooden clappers in one hand, and the veena in the other, he is often portrayed as a real troublemaker, carrying gossip and rumours between gods and wreaking havoc in the process. His entry into any scene in the celestial realm is preceded by the words 'Narayana! Narayana!' Those familiar with Narada's divine escapades are aware that this is cue for much mischief and hilarity to ensue. Let us see what mischief he cooks up in this story.*

Trouble was brewing in the heavens.

Brahma sighed and stroked his long white beard as the thunderous strains of his wife's veena rumbled through the air. Saraswati was angry and he had no idea what he could do to make her feel better.

Vishnu quietly slipped away, hoping Lakshmi would not catch sight of him. She was furiously plucking at the petals of a lotus, muttering something under her breath. He definitely did not want to be at the receiving end of her bad mood.

Shiva watched Parvati cautiously as she stomped about Kailasa in an awful temper. He loved his wife very much indeed, but even he—the fiery Nataraja—knew better than to talk to her when she was in this mood.

The trinity met for a quick conference.

'Any idea what has got them so angry?' Shiva asked. 'I'm afraid to even ask Parvati anything.'

Vishnu laughed. 'You're the one who does the *Tandav*, and you are afraid of your wife?'

Shiva glowered. 'You're a fine one to talk. I bet you haven't said a word to Lakshmi either!'

Before Vishnu could retort, Brahma intervened.

'Boys, I don't think we need to start yet another fight among ourselves. We need to fix this angry-goddess thing before it gets out of hand, and we are all tossed out of our homes.'

Shiva and Vishnu paused, taking in what Brahma said. Then they both nodded in agreement.

'There's only one person I can think of who can fix this for us,' said Vishnu. 'Narada.'

'Excellent choice,' said Shiva, snapping his fingers. 'If anyone can resolve this, it's him.'

'I agree,' Brahma said as he stroked his beard. 'Let's call him.'

Narada cleared his throat nervously just as his mother, Saraswati, paused in her thunderous veena-playing. This was his first stop, and he hoped that his plan would work well.

'*Narayana! Narayana!*' He called out cheerfully.

Saraswati frowned at the disturbance, but when she saw who it was, her brow cleared.

'Oh hello, dear son,' she said. 'Where do you disappear every time I want to discuss something? What brings you here?'

Narada bowed in obeisance. 'Pardon my vanishing acts, respected Mother. You know how busy things are in heaven—I'm in demand everywhere! In fact, I'm on my way to Ganesha's birthday party and thought of checking in on you.'

Saraswati flashed him an indulgent smile, looking placated.

'Umm...was that really you playing the veena? I must say I have never heard this kind of music from you before!'

'Oh!' Saraswati flushed. 'Yes, I was experimenting with something new.'

'Really?' Narada raised a brow, concealing a grin. 'It sounded more like you were furiously twanging on the poor instrument.'

'Umm...', Saraswati looked flushed.

'Are you angry, mother? It's not like you at all. Anything you'd like to share?' Narada prodded slyly.

Saraswati sighed, then shrugged.

'OK, I'll tell you. It's just that I've been hearing all these whispers about Lakshmi and Parvati, and it's beginning to get under my skin.'

'What whispers?'

The goddess plucked at the golden border of her white silk sari nervously.

'The rumours that they are more powerful than me. Better than me.'

'Oh.' Narada sat down on a bench, looking thoughtful.

'What do you think, Narada? You think those two are really better than me? I mean, I am the goddess of learning, of education, of wisdom. What can anyone do without knowledge, tell me? How can anyone say that I am not the most powerful?' Her upturned chin showed defiance.

Narada pursed his lips and tapped a finger on his chin. He knew better than to invoke his mother's wrath, but he couldn't help being frank.

'Well, Goddess Lakshmi is the goddess of wealth. And Goddess Parvati, the goddess of strength...' he trailed.

Saraswati's eyes grew wide in surprise, then narrowed in anger.

'Really?' she snapped. '*You*, of all people, should know that knowledge is the root of all power.'

Narada shrugged, and Saraswati flew into a rage.

'You know what?' Her tone was icy. 'I think you should go now. And don't ever visit again.'

Narada rose and smiled at her. He folded his hands. 'Mother, shall we discuss this later?'

Saraswati glared at him. Narada flinched.

'All right, all right, I will leave.' The sage quietly picked up the clappers, then paused. 'You know, it would be good to remember that the proof of the pudding is in the eating. Now, if you ask me, Vanapur is the perfect place to prove this. That place is in dire straits and could really use some help. But who am I to advise you?' Narada shrugged and vanished into the misty clouds invoking Narayana's name multiple times.

Saraswati strummed the veena's strings in a pensive mood. She would show him. Yes, she would show her mischief-monger of a son—and the entire universe—who was the most powerful goddess in the cosmos! She would be the one to transform Vanapur and make it the most powerful kingdom in the world by blessing them with all the knowledge in the world.

She began playing her veena with renewed determination, the music sounding like a battle-cry.

'*Narayana! Narayana*! Leave that poor flower alone, Goddess Lakshmi. What harm did it ever do you?'

Lakshmi looked at the shredded lotus petals strewn around her lap, then looked up to see Narada smiling at her.

'Hello Narada,' she swept the lotus bits from her lap to the floor and rose. 'What brings you here?'

'Oh, I was just passing by, on my way from Mother's abode.'

Lakshmi made a face.

'I'm sure my neighbour was crowing about her own prowess. Let me tell you—I am the most powerful goddess. With just a snap of my fingers, I can bestow more wealth than you can imagine upon anyone I favour. And with immense wealth comes immense power. No one can ever dispute that. Not even Saraswati or Parvati.'

'Ah! So that's what's been eating at you and making you destroy those lovely lotuses.'

Narada said, his eyes twinkling.

'You agree with me?' Lakshmi demanded, cocking a brow at him.

'Hmmm. Let me see. Goddess Saraswati is the goddess of knowledge, and with immense knowledge comes immense power. Goddess Parvati is the goddess of strength, and with immense strength comes immense power. So, I don't really see the point you're making, you know.' Narada shrugged.

Lakshmi's eyes flashed with fury.

'You know what, Narada? I don't need you, a wandering minstrel, to endorse me. I think you should leave now for your own safety.'

'Of course, of course, Goddess Lakshmi.' Narada raised a placating hand. 'Who am I indeed? No one who needs to be convinced, who needs real proof to believe you, right? You know, Vanapur is the perfect place to prove yourself. It's in such a bad condition that it sorely needs help... All right, all right, don't fly into a rage, I'll show myself out.' He quietly retreated from Lakshmi's abode, pausing momentarily to admire the beautiful lotuses blooming in her pond.

Lakshmi watched the sage leave, her anger unabated. He needed proof, did he? Well, she would prove it beyond doubt that she was the most powerful goddess. Who better than her to transform Vanapur into the mightiest kingdom ever by showering all the wealth in the world on it? Not Saraswati or Parvati—she would do it.

'*Narayana! Narayana*! I thought it was Lord Shiva doing the Tandav again,' a voice stopped Parvati in her tracks. She whirled around and saw Narada smiling at her.

'What are you doing here?' She scowled at him. 'I thought I had made it clear to my guards that I didn't want any visitors.'

'Well, your guards didn't do a great job of stopping me,' Narada shrugged. 'What's got you in such a temper, dear Goddess?'

'Don't you dear me!' Parvati huffed. 'I've had enough of people bowing and scraping and dear-ing me just because I am Shiva's wife. Tell me honestly, do you not think I am goddess enough to be worshipped in my own right? I mean, I am the goddess of strength, the most powerful goddess! Why do people think Lakshmi and Saraswati are better than me? You know that I'm the best!'

'Oh, you do have a good point, my dear *Devi*,' said Narada in a patronizing tone, making Parvati scowl even more. 'But you know, *Devi* Lakshmi is the goddess of wealth and that makes her really powerful. Mother Saraswati is the goddess of knowledge, and everyone knows that knowledge is power. Why would you think that you're the most powerful?' His eyes twinkled with mischief. Oh, how he thrived when the beautiful goddesses—or anyone for that matter—were sparring.

Parvati stamped her foot in rage.

'You...you...!' she spluttered. 'You need to just leave right now if you don't want me to curse or maim you.'

'That was an honest question, *Devi* Parvati,' Narada spread his hands. 'You need to prove that you are the most powerful. That's all I'm saying. And if you ask me, Vanapur is the perfect place, it is in the most terrible state and can only heal with divine intervention...'

'Just go!' Parvati pointed to the exit, quivering in anger. 'Just go right now.'

Narada bowed and floated away in the clouds, looking forward to the delicacies that awaited him at Ganesha's birthday celebrations. Parvati stomped away to her favourite cave hidden in the rugged crevices of Mount Kailasa. He needed proof, did he? She'd show him. She'd show him and the entire universe that she was the most powerful goddess without question. She would make Vanapur the greatest kingdom of all by making it the strongest of all kingdoms in the world. That would settle this silly argument without question!

Vanapur was a little kingdom in dire straits. The king was dying and he had no heir. The court was rife with speculation, the citizens felt hopeless and the kingdom was poised on the brink of a complete breakdown.

It did not help that Narada had slyly mentioned Vanapur to the three goddesses, even if it was just in passing. Their focus was now lasered on this little kingdom, and they were determined to make it the most powerful kingdom ever, each vowing to do this in her own way.

Saraswati rubbed her hands in glee. She had identified her victim...er...person. He was a mute beggar, begging on the streets near the temple.

'I bless you with the light of knowledge to lead you from the darkness.' She intoned as she blessed him. 'You will henceforth be known as Vidyapati.'

Her benediction had immediate effect. The mute person burst into song and rushed into the temple, composing verses on the glory of Mother Saraswati on the spot. Crowds gathered around him, astonished and impressed.

Lakshmi could not help but notice the hullabaloo around Vidyapati. She was irritated, and determined to make her move. It helped that the dying king had sent out an elephant with a garland, announcing that whoever the elephant garlanded would become the next king or queen.

'Let's see. Not him. Not him. Oh, I know. Her!' Lakshmi chortled with glee.

A starving beggar girl who was the poorest of the poor was curled up on the street, hungry and cold.

'I bless you with all the wealth in the world,' Lakshmi intoned. 'You will henceforth be known as Vanadevi.'

The poor girl sat up in alarm when an elephant marched right up to her and threw a garland around her neck. Suddenly the streets were filled with chants.

'All hail the queen! All hail the queen!'

The girl could not believe her eyes. Was she dreaming? If so, this was the best dream ever.

Here she was: being transported to the royal palace, being dressed in silks and adorned in gold, being treated to the most scrumptious feast ever. This was even beyond her dreams; she was now really the queen!

'Take me to the temple,' she said. 'I need to worship Goddess Lakshmi and give her my thanks.'

The temple was filled with people listening to Vidyapati's on-the-spot compositions. The crowd quickly made way for the queen.

'I've heard about you,' Vanadevi said to Vidyapati. 'Let me see how good you are. Can you compose something on the spot praising me?'

'Never!' said Vidyapati fiercely. 'I compose only in praise of Mother Saraswati.'

'How dare you disobey me?' Vanadevi cried. 'Do you know who I am?'

'Yes, I know. You are the queen. But Mother Saraswati is above all queens.'

'I could just snap my fingers and have my guards throw you into the dungeons this very moment!' said Vanadevi angrily.

'I don't care,' said Vidyapati, drawing himself up. 'I will compose only in praise of Mother Saraswati.'

Vanadevi turned away in a huff and threw herself in her chariot. How dare this stupid man talk to her like this? In her anger she pulled hard at the reins. Her horses grew startled and began galloping at high speed. This was not good at all. The queen was in danger. People began screaming in fright as the chariot sped through the streets.

Parvati scoffed at her competitors' efforts. Really? Converting a mute into a genius? A beggar into a queen? She could do so much better. As she scanned Vanapur, her eyes zeroed in on a man cowering in fear before a mouse. There! That was the perfect candidate.

'I bless you with all the power in the world!' Parvati intoned. 'You will henceforth beknown as Veera.'

Veera's body straightened till he stood tall and strong, his muscles bulging, his eyes steady.

As the queen's chariot flew down the street, he stood in its way, calm and steady as a rock.

When the chariot drew close, in a trice he had snatched the reins and stopped the horses. He rubbed them down, calming them and talking to them gently.

'You are very brave indeed!' The queen said, once she had caught her breath. 'I want to make you my commander-in-chief. Accompany me to the palace at once.'

'As you wish, Your Highness,' Veera bowed.

Vanadevi had not forgotten about Vidyapati and his insulting behaviour. She invited him to the court and even made him a royal scribe in an effort to influence him, but he would not compose anything in praise of her. Their arguments in court were beginning to become a royal embarrassment.

One day, Veera had had enough.

He staged a coup and took over the kingdom, throwing both Vidyapati and Vanadevi into prison. He began to rule with an iron fist, and the kingdom of Vanapur sank again into the depths of despair. Things had never looked so bad before.

Narada waited on the outskirts of Vanapur for the goddesses. He had set up a special meeting with them. An angry Lakshmi arrived first, followed by a fuming Parvati and an indifferent Saraswati. They did not look each other in the eye, glaring at Narada instead.

'So,' Narada began. 'I've been following the proceedings in Vanapur. Forgive me, *Devis*, but it looks like none of you could prove your point.'

'What nonsense!' Lakshmi sprang up, furious. 'I made Vanadevi queen!'

'And look where she is,' Saraswati smirked. 'In the dungeons.'

'As is your Vidyapati,' Parvati laughed. 'My Veera is the only one who's come out on top.'

'And see how the kingdom has been ruined,' scoffed Lakshmi.

'Have you come to laugh at us?' Saraswati turned to Narada in anger. 'Is that what this meeting is all about? Pointing out that none of us are good enough?'

'What do you think?' asked Narada.

The three goddesses looked at each other.

'This should have worked. Veera is strong enough to command the army; Vanadevi should have continued as queen; and Vidyapati should have continued as chief counsel,' Parvati mused.

'Then what went wrong?' Lakshmi asked. 'Vanapur should have been the best kingdom in the whole world if things had gone the right way.'

Narada looked at the three of them with a quiet smile.

'It's us,' Saraswati said, realization dawning on her. 'We should have worked together.'

'You know, I think you're right. We were so focused on proving ourselves that we let our egos get the better of us,' Parvati agreed.

'You're right,' nodded Lakshmi. 'Wealth, power, and

knowledge would have been put to the best use if we had worked together, and not as rivals to prove a point.'

The three of them turned to Narada.

'This is all your doing, isn't it?' asked Saraswati.

'You tricked us into this,' added Parvati.

'You wanted to teach us a lesson,' concluded Lakshmi.

Narada looked startled. 'Me, a wandering singing bard, teaching you goddesses a lesson?

*Narayana! Narayana!*'

'Come on,' Saraswati laughed. 'Don't play the idiot.'

'It's time to confess to your clever trick,' Parvati smiled.

'You don't stand a chance against the three of us!' Lakshmi's threat was clearly harmless since she was grinning.

'I don't,' agreed Narada. 'You three together are a force to reckon with. I'm glad you are together.'

'You, my dear son, are no humble wandering singing bard. You are a genius.' Saraswati laughed. The other two goddesses joined her.

'All with your blessings always, my dear goddesses,' bowed Narada. '*Narayana! Narayana*!'

As the goddesses fell deep into a discussion on how to make Vanapur the best kingdom ever, Narada walked away with a smile on his face. His job was done.

# With Best Compliments

*Who hasn't heard of Mullah Nasruddin? His stories are famous all over Asia, from Turkey through China to India. Mullah Nasruddin sometimes appears to be a fool or dimwit, but, make no mistake, he is very clever.*

*Did you know that there is an International Nasreddin Hodja Festival that is celebrated annually in Akşehir, Türkiye, between 5 and 10 July?*

One fine day, the mayor of the town where Nasruddin lived decided to host a grand party.

'It will be the best party this town has ever seen,' he declared to his wife. 'We will put up the most expensive and beautiful decorations in our grand hall. We will host the most fantastic feast with the most mouth-watering delicacies that have ever been served in this town. And we will wear the most gorgeous clothes ever designed. Everyone will be stunned and this party will be talked about for generations to come. We will go down in history!'

The mayor's wife sighed and left the room. She knew her husband prided himself on his excellent taste and would leave no stone unturned to host this magnificent party he was talking about. Of course, that meant a great deal of extra work for her. She would have to hire extra hands to help with the decorations; she would have to go to the next town to hire the great chef, Badshah, who had a reputation for being brilliant but picky; she would have to go shopping for the finest silks and satins, and then ensure that the super-busy tailor Muzaffar delivered their best-fit suits and skirts on time. She could not waste a moment more, she had to start work right away.

Meanwhile, the mayor ordered the boy who worked as his clerk to run and get some of the finest paper and inks. He then sat and dictated the text to his scribe, who then created the invitations with great care and concentration, making sure the calligraphy was perfect.

As soon as the invitations began to be distributed, the party became the talk of the town.

'Did you hear that the great chef, Badshah is catering for the party? I won't miss it for the world! I've heard his dishes are so mouth-watering, some of the guests end up eating even the plate. I think I will have to fast two days in advance to do justice to his cooking.'

'Oh, I can't wait to see what finery everyone will be wearing. I will wear my new green skirt with gold embroidery. Dear husband, give me your money bag, I will need to buy matching jewellery.'

The shops in town were suddenly abuzz with customers, all vying with each other to buy the best clothes and shoes and jewels.

As Mullah Nasruddin sauntered past the street where men sat at little tables and played parcheesi, one of the men hailed him.

'Hey Mullah!' He called out. 'We haven't seen you in a while. Where were you?'

'Oh, I was out of town on an errand,' Mullah Nasruddin replied. 'What's going on? The whole town seems to be in a tizzy.'

'You haven't got the invitation yet?' the man laughed. 'To the party of the year—nay, the century—that the mayor is hosting?'

'I got the invitation all right,' Mullah replied. 'And what a fine invitation it was. The finest calligraphy on the finest paper with the finest ink.'

'So, are you all set? All ready with your finest clothes and a good appetite to wine and dine with the first citizen of this town?'

'My appetite is always good,' replied Mullah with a laugh. 'I don't think I will have any problems eating at the feast. But finest clothes? Hmmm...'

'Well, if you want my advice, you better get them soon, before all the shops in town run out. They are raising the prices every day too, so you'd better hurry.'

Mullah smiled and nodded before departing. What the man had said made him think a great deal. As he wandered the streets of the town, he moved further and further away from the busy shopping areas, till he reached a small lane. A couple of street vendors had set up their stalls and Mullah browsed through their wares. There were beautiful hand-crafted wooden toys and corner tables, skilfully woven tapestries and scarves, artistic pots and mugs, and ornate turbans.

Mullah picked up one of the turbans. It was a deep red, with gold trimmings and intricate embroidery. It looked quite grand even though it was made of rather cheap material and cheap thread.

He placed it on his head and the vendor immediately produced a mirror.

'*Wah! Wah!* You look like a king, I swear!'

Mullah laughed heartily. 'Stop with the flattery,' he

said. ‘I know exactly how I look with this turban on my head. Like a fool on my way to another fool’s party. Tell me, how much is this?’

When the vendor quoted the very low figure, Mullah was aghast.

‘You are charging this much for this?’

‘Sahib, I can lower the price if you want, but only by a little. I have to eat and feed my family too. If I sell it for any less, we will probably all starve.’

‘My good man!’ Mullah slapped the vendor on his back. ‘I was not trying to bargain. I was actually surprised that you are selling this for such a low price. Who does the work on this turban?’

‘My wife, Sahib,’ the vendor replied. ‘She is very talented and can do the most intricate designs in the shortest time. Then I make the turban.’

‘My dear sir,’ Mullah Nasruddin replied. ‘Both of you are selling your skills a little too short. I will give

you double the price. And I bet you that I can sell this turban for more than ten times the price. And what's more, I bet you I will sell it to the mayor himself!'

'Sahib, you are too kind!' The vendor cried out in astonishment. 'I cannot cheat you—please pay me the right price, no need to pay double. And as for selling this to the mayor, well, good luck with that. The first citizen of the town is probably used to the best of the best, and he will identify this cheap turban for exactly what it is. I am a poor man and I do not gamble, so I won't take you up on your bet. But do feel free to come and let me know the result if you succeed.'

Mullah laughed merrily and paid the grateful vendor a little extra. He took the turban and went home. His party dress was now ready.

The day of the party dawned bright and sunny. Everything was ready and perfect. The mayor's wife had checked and double-checked with every single helping hand. She had even dared to peep into the kitchen and was relieved to see a cheerful Badshah, whistling as he shouted instructions., He was stirring, and whipping up all sorts of bubbling concoctions on the stoves.

She called out to her maids who did her hair, and then helped her into her elaborate pink skirt, which had gold trimming and glittering sequins all over. She reddened her lips, dusted some rouge on her cheeks, and outlined her eyes carefully with kohl. She adjusted her golden netted veil and put on the heavy golden jewellery studded with semi-precious stones. As she slipped on her golden shoes, she couldn't help thinking that she hadn't got so dressed up even on her own wedding day.

The mayor was waiting for her outside the grand

party hall. He looked particularly dashing in a navy blue pathan suit with a dull gold waistcoat and matching shoes. His pink turban matched her outfit.

'You are looking like a *pari*, a completely gorgeous fairy, my love,' he said with a smile as he kissed her hand.

'You are looking very handsome yourself, my dear husband,' his wife replied, with a twinkle in her eye.

'Come, let us go and get this party started,' the mayor said, leading her into the hall by the hand. It was already quite crowded and people were still coming in. They were greeted very enthusiastically by the folks, who ooh-ed and aah-ed over every little arrangement, making the mayor beam with happiness. His wife heaved a sigh of relief.

By the time Mullah Nasruddin joined the party, everyone was having a fabulous time. There was music and dance, the exotic and delectable dishes kept coming, and the fashion statements made by the partygoers made eyes goggle and jaws drop. It was indeed turning out to be the party of the century.

After doing the rounds and greeting friends, Mullah Nasruddin made a beeline for the mayor. He first sought out the mayor's wife and congratulated her on the grand success. Her cheeks were flushed and eyes were shining. She thanked him profusely for joining them and for his kind comments.

He then met the mayor.

'Mullah Nasruddin!' The boisterous mayor slapped him heartily on the back, no doubt having had a drink too many. 'Long time since I've seen you around. Where have you been?'

'Oh, I was out of town on some errands. I'm glad I made it back in time for this grand party,' Mullah Nasruddin replied, trying to get his hand back from the mayor's firm grip.

'Yes, yes, I'm certainly glad you are back in time for this,' the mayor said. 'Have some of the fine food and enjoy yourself. This is a once-in-a-lifetime event, right?'

'Of course,' Mullah Nasruddin nodded with a smile, adjusting his turban. 'I have no doubt that this will be remembered for generations to come. All credit to you, of course, you have such excellent taste in everything.'

'Of course, of course,' the mayor beamed so widely that his smile threatened to split his face. As his gaze wandered to Mullah's turban, he said generously, 'You have good taste too, Mullah. Just look at your turban. Such a masterpiece! Such a grand, fine turban!'

'See, you have just proved my point,' Mullah laughed. 'Only a person with such discerning taste would be able to see that this turban is outstanding. It was made by a master turban-maker, and it is the only one of its kind.'

'Is that right?' The mayor was now curious. 'Who is this master turban-maker? I want to meet him and get myself a turban too.'

'Oh, he doesn't stay in one place, so it is very difficult to trace him. I was just lucky that I met him at the right time.'

The mayor's face fell.

'Oh, that's too bad,' he said. 'I really want a turban like yours.'

'You know what?' Mullah Nasruddin took his turban off. 'You should take this. You are a person with such good taste. This turban is wasted on me. You ought to be the one who owns it.'

'Oh, I couldn't just take it like that,' the mayor said, getting a bit flustered. A crowd had now gathered around them, and people were listening to the entire exchange.

'Why not?' Mullah Nasruddin looked surprised.

'No, you must have paid a good sum for this, I can't just take it for free,' the mayor replied.

'If that is how you feel, then why don't you just pay me a token sum?' Mullah Nasruddin persisted. 'I don't need to be paid the exact price.'

'What is the exact price?' One of the men from the crowd around them chimed in.

Others also chimed in. 'Yes, yes, if this turban is such a masterpiece, tell us exactly how much you paid for it.'

Mullah Nasruddin shrugged and told them. Just as he had promised the street vendor, he named a price that was ten times what he had actually paid.

Jaws dropped.

'No way!'

'You must be insane!'

'There's no way any turban could cost this much.'

'You must have got cheated.'

Voices rose from the crowd around them.

The man who had asked Mullah Nasruddin for the exact price turned to the mayor.

'Sir, please excuse my frankness, but honestly, this turban just cannot be worth this much. I have seen many beautiful and wonderful turbans that cost just a fraction of the price. Please don't be fooled by

Mullah Nasruddin. He must just be pulling your leg.'

Everyone nodded in agreement.

The mayor turned to Mullah Nasruddin.

'What do you say, Mullah? Everyone seems to think that your turban is overpriced. It is way too expensive, don't you think?'

Mullah Nasruddin shrugged.

'I respect everyone, and they are entitled to their own opinions—who am I to disagree? However, the price I quoted is just what I bought it for. Surely someone who has such exquisite taste as yourself knows that such items are priceless. In fact, you are the only one in the world that I can think of who deserves such an incomparable turban, because you are the only one who has the good taste to appreciate it. Just look at this party—how tasteful it is, whether it be the decorations, the food, or even your dress. I honestly believe that you are the only person with taste impeccable enough to appreciate my turban.'

The mayor's chest expanded so much with pride that he was in danger of exploding.

'You are right, Mullah. No item is too pricey for a man of good taste. I will pay you the exact amount.'

'I bow to your sensitivities,' Mullah Nasruddin bowed elaborately and handed over the turban. 'This is all yours, I believe.'

'Just wait right here, I will hand you the money in front of all these people who will serve as witnesses.' The mayor hurried away, carrying the turban carefully in his hands.

The next day, the street vendor could not believe his eyes when Mullah Nasruddin handed over a heavy bag of gold to him.

'You really sold the turban for ten times the price?' he asked, his eyes wide with astonishment.

'The turban may be worth only what you sold it to me for, but the price of a compliment to the mayor is worth ten times more,' Mullah Nasruddin laughed. 'I just recovered the price of the compliment for you.'

The party of the century was unfortunately soon forgotten, but the story of Mullah Nasruddin and the turban was told and retold for generations to come.

## A Close Shave

*Kitsune are shape-shifting foxes in Japanese folklore. They possess supernatural abilities and can be both good and bad. There are many beliefs surrounding the kitsune, and one of them is the belief that they can be tricksters and are able to deceive human beings. As with all such stories, the outcomes can range from hilarious mix-ups to dire consequences. After all, the supernatural is no laughing matter, is it?*

The dinner party was in full swing. People were having a great time, the food was superb, the drinks were even better, and the conversation was spectacular. But as is wont to happen at such gatherings, a fierce argument had broken out, and at the centre of it was Tokutaro, the carpenter. He was a very stubborn man who would not bend to anyone else's point of view.

'You have no idea about the world, Tokutaro,' one of the men laughed. 'There are things that are beyond what you and I can imagine, things beyond our control. You say that it is impossible for foxes to trick humans, but what do you say to those who have seen it with their own eyes? Are they lying?'

'In fact,' one of the other men interjected, 'right here in Maki Moor, we've heard of so many men getting tricked by those foxes, haven't we?' The Moor was the name given to the wild and remote marshlands near

Maki, a small Japanese town. In Japanese folklore, this mysterious stretch of land was associated with supernatural events or beings, especially foxes (*kitsune*).

'Yes,' the first man replied. 'Nearly thirty cases such have been reported, and no one has been able to prove otherwise—that it was something other than the trickery of the foxes. What do you say to that?'

Tokutaro drained his goblet and put it down with a flourish.

'You know, you are all idiots. Those men who said they were fooled by the foxes—they are idiots too. Nothing on earth will persuade me that foxes wield so much power that they can deceive us. Nothing.'

'Very well,' the second man said with a sly smile. 'You leave us no choice. Let us have a wager. You go to Maki Moor and spend the night there. And if you come home tomorrow without any incident or accident, we will believe you.'

'If it's a wager, we need to agree on a forfeit,' said Tokutaro grinning. 'How about you pay me in *sake* and fish? Five barrels of *sake* and fish worth a thousand coins?'

'That's fine, but remember that if you lose, you need to give *us* five barrels of wine and a thousand coins worth of fish!'

Tokutaro laughed heartily. 'Done. You folks are all idiots. Mark my words: tomorrow at this time, I will be wining and dining on my winnings, and you will all be ruing the day you wagered against me.'

'Very well,' said the men, 'let us drink to that!'

They all raised their glasses and with a loud cheer, they toasted Tokutaro. The party wound up soon after that, and as the last of the guests trickled out, it was time for Tokutaro to leave for the eerie Maki Moor.

Off he went, wrapping himself in a shawl to keep warm, and holding a lantern to see his path during the night. The Maki Moor was on the outskirts of the village and it was dark and murky. Tokutaro was not afraid, however. He strode confidently into the night.

Just as he reached the Maki Moor, a fox ran across his path and disappeared into the bamboo grove that hugged the edge of the moor.

'Aha, there goes the fox,' Tokutaro muttered to himself. 'I have seen it now, so I know that it will try to trick me soon. But I am prepared for any trick it tries. It had better watch out—Tokutaro will not be deceived so easily!'

He passed the bamboo grove and headed towards the interior of the moor. As he rounded the corner, he could suddenly hear the sound of footsteps behind him. A shiver ran down his spine. What—or who—could be following him?

'Master Tokutaro!' A gentle female voice called out to him and he stopped in his tracks. Slowly turning, he beheld a beautiful young girl. She was petite and her hair was sleek and pulled back into a ponytail. She was wearing a furry coat of sorts over an expensive-looking kimono. Her almond-shaped slanted eyes resembled those of a fox. What on earth was she doing out here in the night? Was it...the fox?

She drew closer to him, and he realized it was the daughter-in-law of the village chief.

'Oh, hello,' he said with a tentative smile. 'What are you doing out here in the night, umm..?' He couldn't remember her name, although they had met on a couple of occasions when he had done some carpentry work in her house.

'I'm Aiko,' she said with a shy smile. 'I need to go back to my father's house urgently, which is across the Maki Moor. I know it looks strange that I didn't bring along any companions, but everyone is busy with the harvest and I didn't want to disturb them. I will anyway just be gone for a day. I thought if I went tonight and returned tomorrow night, it would be perfect.' The woman lowered her eyes, seemingly too timid to meet Tokutaro's gaze.

Tokutaro nodded, but he was not convinced at all. There was no way the headman would have agreed to send his daughter-in-law alone. This must be the fox trying to trick him into something! Very well, two can play at this game, he thought. He would go along with this deception till he could be sure. Then he would confront the fox and call his bluff.

'No problem at all, milady,' he said bowing. 'I will accompany you to your father's house.'

'That is really kind of you, Master Tokutaro,' she said, again with a shy smile. 'I am grateful for your kind offer to accompany me. I have crossed the Maki Moor alone in the daytime, but at night, everything looks so much more frightening. Thank you so much!'

Tokutaro waved his hand, dismissing her show of gratitude. No need to put on such an act, he thought, smirking silently to himself.

Tokutaro and Aiko began making their way across the moor. The narrow path was lined with thorny bushes and their robes kept getting caught on the thorns, which pricked them as they slowly made their way through the moor. Owls hooted in the distance and bats swooped dangerously low, their wings almost touching Tokutaro and Aiko's faces. The stars twinkled in the distance and a stiff cold wind blew across the moor, its icy fingers reaching through their clothes and making them shiver. Still, Tokutaro and the young lady walked steadily into the night.

Hours later, the pale fingers of dawn crept through the morning sky as the young lady and Tokutaro reached their destination. Her father was tying firewood into bundles and her mother was drawing water from the well. When they saw her, they dropped whatever they were doing and rushed to the girl.

'Oh daughter, what brings you here? Is everything alright?' Her mother embraced her and ran her hands over the girl's face to make sure nothing bad had happened.

'Nothing has happened to me, mother,' the young lady replied with a laugh. 'I am so glad to see that both of you are doing well. I got news that you had taken ill, and I was so worried. That is why I rushed over to your house, even though I had to travel across the Maki Moor by night. I was fortunate enough to come across this brave man who agreed to accompany me. All thanks to him!'

'This is so strange!' the mother wondered. 'Why would you get news that I had taken ill? I don't understand this at all. But I am so glad that you came. It has been so many months since I last saw you. Come, let me make something nice for you to eat while you wash up. You too, young man. You are our guest. We are deeply grateful that you brought our daughter home safely.'

The mother took the girl inside the house.

The father turned to Tokutaro. 'Thank you, kind sir,' he said, bowing low. 'I will forever be indebted to you for making sure that my daughter reached her mother's house safe and sound.'

'I would not be so quick in thanking me, sir,' Tokutaro answered with a smirk. 'Everything might not be as it seems.'

'Why do you say that?' the father asked, puzzled.

'Well, when I was entering the moor, I saw a fox running into a bamboo grove. When I reached the other side, I found your daughter. I am convinced that she is a *kitsune* trying to pull a fast one on us. I accompanied her all right, because I did not want the *kitsune* to suspect that I already knew the trick it was pulling on me. But trust me, this girl is not your daughter. And if you give me some time, I will prove it to you.'

'Oh, is that so?' The father's jaw dropped. 'I must thank you then, for telling me about this. If the girl is indeed not my daughter but the *kitsune*, I will be even more grateful to you.' Aiko's father had been duped by a *kitsune* years ago and the episode still haunted him.

Tokutaro waved a dismissive hand. 'Not at all, Sir. Now, if you can get your wife out of the house, I can proceed to unmask the *kitsune*.'

'Sure, sure,' the old man agreed and hurried into the house. In a few minutes, he had dragged his wife out, but she was not happy.

'What is this that you want to tell me, husband?' she

grumbled. 'I need to start making the dumplings if we are to have any breakfast at a decent hour.'

'Shhh, wife! Listen to what this young man has to say, it is important.'

Tokutaro then proceeded to tell the wife the same story he had told the husband. But it did not elicit the same reaction at all.

'Are you crazy?' The wife huffed. 'That girl is my daughter, I swear. I don't believe your ridiculous story and you can leave her alone, thank you very much.'

'Woman!' Her husband said, shocked. 'Are you saying that this young man is lying to us?'

'I don't care if he is lying or not. All I know is that the girl inside my house is my very own daughter—our own flesh and blood!' She glared at her husband.

'Sir,' Tokutaro gently interjected. 'If you could just give me a few minutes alone with your daughter, I will unmask the *kitsune*.'

'No, Sir! You will leave her alone!' The woman yelled, even as her husband held her hands to her back and dragged her away.

'Go ahead,' he gestured to Tokutaro. 'Do what you need to.'

Tokutaro entered the house. There was a nice fire going, and pots and pans were all readied for cooking. The young girl washed up and came looking for her mother.

'Oh, Sir, it's you! Where is my mother?' Aiko asked, when she saw Tokutaro.

Tokutaro moved towards her, and, much to Aiko's horror, suddenly seized her hand.

'Tell me the truth!' he hissed under his breath. 'You

are *kitsune*, aren't you? Trying to trick us all, eh?'

The young girl's face grew pale with fear.

'*K-kitsune*?' she stammered. 'Wh-what are you talking about?'

Tokutaro twisted her hands behind her back till she screamed in pain.

'*What are you talking about?*' He mimicked her. 'Don't try to trick me, I am too clever for the likes of you!' He breathed into her face and pushed her. 'Confess! Tell me the truth! You *are kitsune*, are you not?'

'No...no...please let me go,' the girl sobbed. 'I am *not kitsune*, I am their daughter.' She said, pointing in the general direction of her parents.

'No way!' Tokutaro pushed her again, and she slipped out of his hands. He stared in horror as she fell right into the fire. He turned pale with understanding.

'No, no!' He shouted and tried to pull her out. But it was too late—the flames had engulfed her. She ran out of the house, aflame and shrieking in pain, and collapsed in a lifeless heap right in front of her parents.

Aiko's mother hurled curses at Tokutaro.

'I told you she was not *kitsune*! I told you she was our daughter. Wha...what did you do, you evil man?' She collapsed next to her daughter, her breath catching, as she sobbed uncontrollably .

Tokutaro stood frozen and speechless. He had definitely not expected such a turn of events. He had been so consumed by the idea that the *kitsune* was out to trick him that he hadn't for a minute considered that the girl could really be the daughter of the couple standing before him.

The couple was howling in sorrow. Tokutaro hung

his head in shame. What could he do now? He was filled with remorse for his unbecoming conduct. He was a terrible, terrible person who had caused the death of the old couple's daughter. How could he atone for such an awful deed? What could he do or say or offer to make them feel better? Even if he offered to be sentenced to death, he could never bring their daughter back. What was he to do? He stood there in silence, his heart overflowing with guilt and grief.

Soon a crowd gathered outside the house. When they heard what had happened, they became enraged.

'We need to punish this rascal,' they shouted. 'He needs to be produced before our chief and justice needs to be served.'

They bound Tokutaro with ropes and began kicking and slapping him. He bore it all because he knew he deserved it. Just as they were about to drag him to the chief's house, they were stopped by a sonorous voice.

'Is all well here? What has happened?'

The crowd parted to reveal a priest who was accompanied by his disciple. He stood tall and noble, his broad forehead and calm gaze instantly silencing the fierce hate cries against Tokutaro emanating from the mob.

'My lord,' the father came forward and fell to his knees. 'We thought that this young man had done us a great service by accompanying our daughter, Aiko, across the moor at night. But he turned out to be an evil man. He caused her to fall into the fire and die. all because he thought she was a *kitsune* and was deceiving us. We are taking him to our chief. Justice *must* be served.'

Tokutaro raised his eyes to the priest and beseeched him with tearful eyes.

'I never intended to kill her, O Great One! It was an accident, I swear. My only mistake was that I took her to be a *kitsune*—as you know, they are shape-shifting tricksters and are known to deceive people. I... I was convinced that Aiko was a *kitsune* and wanted to unmask her. I had no other intention, I promise. Please save me.' Tokutaro hung his head in shame.

The priest looked at Tokutaro long and hard.

'Hmm...if I save you, will you agree to be my disciple? Walk with me on my long journeys, learn what I teach, eat what I give you, and sleep where I tell you to? It will be arduous, but this is what I demand if I am to save your life.'

'Whatever you say, Sire,' Tokutaro clasped his hands in prayer. 'If you save my life, *my* life is yours. Do what you will with it.'

The priest sighed. He turned to the father and placed a kindly hand on his shoulder.

'Listen to what I say, dear sir,' he said. 'I understand your grief completely. Losing a daughter is dreadful, and much as you would like this young man to be punished in the most severe way, consider these facts: one, he did accompany your daughter all the way across the moor and brought her home safely; two, he had good intentions; he wanted to save you from the *kitsune*, and hence he attacked her; three, her death was a pure accident; it was not caused deliberately by him. four, even if he were to be sentenced to death, your daughter would not come back to life; five, if he is spared, he has agreed to become my disciple, which means he will only do better in the future. Keeping all these facts in mind, do a good deed, and instead of having the sin of this man's death upon your head, spare him and let him come with me.'

The priest's reasoning set the crowd murmuring. Several folks nodded their heads in agreement, and soon, the voices urging the parents to follow the priest's suggestion grew louder.

The father and mother whispered to each other, and then the mother stepped forward and spoke in a voice choked with emotion.

'Kind Sire, we agree with what you say. One bad incident should not be worsened by another. You may take this young man away and make him your disciple. You have our consent.'

'A wise decision, kind lady,' the priest nodded. He gestured to his companion who knelt and untied the ropes that bound Tokutaro. He stumbled as he tried to rise from the ground. The priest outstretched his hand in support.

'Thank you, thank you!' Tokutaro vigorously bowed low to the couple in gratitude. 'I have caused you inconsolable grief but I promise I will be worthy of your forgiveness someday.'

'As you are aware,' the priest said to Tokutaro, 'you will need to discard your robes and wear the ones that will be given to you. And you will have to shave your head.'

'As you say, kind Sire,' Tokutaro bowed his head.

The entire village watched as the priest's companion shaved Tokutaro's head.

'It is done,' the companion said, stepping backwards

and the crowd burst into laughter upon seeing Tokutaro's bald head.

Bewildered, Tokutaro raised his head. To his utter astonishment he saw that he was kneeling in the middle of the moor. He looked around him and there was not a single person around—not the priest or his disciple or the villagers or the parents of the girl. He put his hands on his head and was startled to find that his head was indeed bereft of hair! Slowly, realization dawned on him. The *kitsune* had deceived him, after all! Aiko, her parents, Aiko's death, the mobs, and the priest had all been an illusion. He had been tricked by the *kitsune*, and how!

Tokutaro returned to his village, a much chastened and humbled man. His friends roared with laughter as he narrated his story. Tokutaro quietly gifted five barrels of *sake* and fish worth a thousand coins to his friend with whom he had a wager.

But Tokutaro had changed. He had lost not just his hair but also his stubbornness. He never grew his hair again, and after a few weeks, he embraced priesthood and began his travels across the land, sharing the lessons of humility and wisdom he had gained from his own experience. Crucially, he never spoke dismissively about the *kitsune* again. Who knows what games these supernatural beings might play if he did?

# Tricking the Dokkaebi

*In Korean folklore and mythology, Dokkaebi are the goblins. They possess supernatural powers, and use these powers to sometimes trick people, or sometimes help them. What makes them unique is that they often possess inanimate objects like brooms. They are also known as formidable wrestlers and cannot resist challenging folks in a match. But can one ever outwit Dokkaebi? Let's find out.*

It was a cold wintry night, and up in the mountains, it was even more chilly. A peasant—let's call him Kim, shivered in his threadbare coat as he piled up firewood and tried to get a warm fire going in his little cottage. The cottage was perched precariously on the mountain slope and was in desperate need of repairs. The roof had many holes that he had patched up with straw and rags and whatever he could find. The walls were thin and creaked dangerously when the strong wind blew.

'If only I had some money to buy some proper timber, I could fix this place up so nicely,' he thought to himself. 'I'd replace the entire roof so that it wouldn't leak, I'd reinforce the walls so that they wouldn't shake so much. I'd get a nice thick blanket, and a warm toasty bed. I'd get some fresh meat and the best cheese. I'd put down a fluffy rug in front of the fireplace and get myself a solid armchair with a footstool so that I could rest my tired legs after a long day.'

He poked the fire and added some more twigs. Then he poured himself a drink and settled down for the night, covering himself with a thin shawl.

Just then, there was a knock on the door. Kim ignored the knock—most probably it was just the wind. He had no friends down at the village, at least no one so close to him that they would seek out his company on this frosty night. But then it sounded once more, and then again, more urgently.

'Who on earth could it be?' Kim wondered, as he padded to the door. He opened it a crack, and peered into the darkness.

A shadowy figure stood outside.

'Who are you?' Kim asked, not opening the door fully. 'What do you want?'

'I am really cold outside,' the figure replied in a low whisper. 'Could I come in and trouble you for a drink?'

Kim hesitated, unsure whether to invite a complete stranger into his home. But what did he have to lose? He didn't have any riches or money, so there was nothing to rob. And he had a stout stick leaning against the wall, so if his visitor tried any tricks, he could easily beat him off. What was the harm in inviting the man in for a drink? At least he would have some company for some time.

He shrugged and opened the door wide.

'Come on in,' he invited. 'I don't have much to offer in the way of food, but I can certainly offer you a drink and some warmth before my fire.'

'Thank you,' the stranger replied, and shuffled into the house. He was much shorter than Kim and seemed to be bent over under his cloak. He sank before the fire with a grateful sigh and accepted the drink that was poured out for him.

Kim kept glancing at the stranger, who seemed rather hairy, with bulging eyes and a rather large mouth.

'So, what brings you to this part of the country?' Kim asked, breaking the silence that had enveloped them.

'I've just been travelling around,' his guest said. His voice was low and hoarse, and he didn't meet Kim's eyes.

'Is that so? Where have you been?'

Perhaps the drink helped the stranger to relax, but as the room grew warmer, he began to talk a lot more with Kim. He told him about all the places he had been to, and the adventures he had had. It was late at night when he finally rose.

'I think I should leave now,' he said. 'It is quite late, and I should not be disturbing you.'

'That's OK, Kim replied. 'You can stay here if you want. I don't have a good bed or a warm blanket to offer, but you are most welcome to stay the night.'

'You are a good man to offer,' the guest said with a smile, and Kim started in surprise. The stranger's teeth were so sharp and long that it gave him quite a fright. 'But I will not stay. Thank you, friend, for a most pleasant evening. If you don't mind, may I drop in tomorrow also? I think I would like to have some company, and I quite enjoyed chatting with you today.'

'Sure,' Kim said, a bit flustered. 'You are most welcome tomorrow.'

The stranger clasped Kim's hands in his, and Kim was startled to see that his nails were long and sharp, almost like claws. He disentangled his hands quickly and smiled at the stranger.

'Good night, then.'

'Good night, my friend.' The stranger walked away and Kim could have sworn that he saw him just disappear into the mist. But he had had much to drink, it was late, and he was sleepy, so when he awoke in the morning, he was not sure if he had really seen what he had seen, or if it was all his imagination.

But all his doubts vanished when he heard a knock on his door that night as well. The stranger had returned, and this time, Kim drank less and kept an alert eye on the visitor. The evening was pretty much a repeat of the previous evening, with his guest regaling him with interesting stories about his travels and then leaving at around midnight.

Soon, this became a pattern, and Kim relaxed. He no longer worried about the stranger, who seemed quite harmless, and just a little lonely. He ignored how hairy the stranger seemed, or how his eyes seemed to bulge even more, or how his sharp teeth and nails gleamed in the firelight quite dangerously. Kim was happy to have found a friend who asked nothing much of him and provided him with so much entertainment. He began to look forward to the cold nights with enthusiasm, enjoying the company of the stranger without much thought.

As time passed, Kim became aware of the weird looks that the villagers kept throwing at him every time he went to the village. They never met his eyes, and looked away hastily whenever he tried to make eye contact. They gradually began moving away from his path, barely talking to him, answering him in monosyllables, and in general, trying to completely avoid him. Kim wondered what the problem was. Was it because he had become such good friends with his guest? Were they envious of him? Or was his guest someone he should be avoiding too? Was there something about him that he didn't know? But Kim dismissed these thoughts as he hurried home every day, eager to catch up with his friend and have a good time, chatting and drinking.

One afternoon, after Kim had finished all his work and was on his way home. he stumbled upon a small rock and fell to the ground. He wasn't hurt, but his hands were all muddy as he had used them to brace himself when he fell. There was a small pool of water just ahead, and he made towards it, so that he could wash his hands clean. When he reached the pool, he bent over the water to rinse his hands. However, he received such a great shock upon seeing his reflection that he jumped backwards and fell on his back.

What was that that he had seen reflected in the water? It could not be! Something had to be wrong with his eyesight. Maybe dust had got into his eyes. He rose slowly and bent over the water again. His jaw dropped in astonishment as he saw his reflection. Was that really him? What had happened? Why did he resemble his visitor so much? Had he always looked like him? And when had his teeth begun to become so sharp? Just like his visitor's teeth! Kim slowly rolled up his sleeves and his pants. Now there was no denying it—his hair had definitely thickened, looking just like his visitor's! Kim glanced down at his nails and was horrified to see that they too were gradually taking on the shape of claws, just like his visitor! No wonder the villagers were running away from him whenever they spotted him. Why had he not realized this earlier?

The more Kim thought about it, the more he realized that there was only one possible explanation. His visitor must be *Dokkaebi*—a goblin possessing supernatural powers. Why had the Dokkaebi befriended him? What trick was he planning to play on Kim? Was he going to turn Kim into a Dokkaebi too?

When Kim reached his home, he paced about, worried sick. What could he do? He couldn't turn away his guest without offending him. God knows what his guest might unleash on him if he got offended.

'There must be some way to end this friendship,' Kim thought desperately, fear gnawing at him. 'How can I make this go away and still survive?'

By the time night fell and his guest arrived as usual, Kim was ready with a plan. He knew he could not afford to have his visitor smell a rat, so he behaved as normally as he could. He brought out the drinks and encouraged his friend to share more of his stories.

After listening to yet another entertaining story, Kim filled their glasses again.

'You know,' he began casually, 'you are indeed the bravest person I have ever known. You have encountered so many ferocious beasts and battled so many brave warriors. Are you afraid of anything at all? I don't have anything to offer as a wager, but I am willing to bet that you don't have an ounce of fear in your body. I wish I could be like you!'

His guest grinned. 'You are wrong, you are very wrong indeed. I *am* afraid of something. And it's good that you didn't place any wager, for you would definitely have lost!'

'Come on, you're just pulling my leg,' Kim scoffed. 'I am not convinced that you are afraid of anything. I dare you to tell me what you are afraid of. Go ahead, tell me. If you don't, I know you have just been lying about being afraid.'

His guest cleared his throat a bit nervously. 'All right, since you insist.' He lowered his voice into a whisper. 'I am very, very scared of blood. I am terrified of it!'

Kim laughed out loud. 'You are just joking, mister. I don't believe you at all. So much for telling the truth!'

'I am not joking; I *am* afraid of blood!' His guest raised his voice in protest.

'Of course, you are not joking,' Kim winked. His heart was thudding violently, and he hoped the other man would not realize just how fearful he was.

'Now it's your turn to tell me what you are afraid of,' his companion poked him in the ribs and smiled. 'Don't think for a moment that I am going to let you off the hook. You have to confess your fear too.'

Kim's thoughts raced. His mouth went dry and his palms grew damp. Perspiration beaded his forehead, and his hand shook as he raised his glass to his lips, barely able to swallow his drink. How could he admit that he was most afraid of the person sitting in front of him? He needed to think of something fast. His gaze fell upon a huge crack in the wall and suddenly an idea struck him.

He turned to his friend and smiled, hiding his nervousness well.

'You see this shack? It's ready to fall to pieces. In truth, it ought to have been torn down, for it is a danger to anyone living here. But you know why I am not doing any repairs? Why I'm not redoing my roof, reinforcing my walls, and making this a place safe?'

His companion looked at him with curiosity gleaming in his eyes and raised an enquiring eyebrow.

'Because I am terrified of *money*!' Kim whispered dramatically. 'I cannot bear to touch money. I get hives if a coin falls near me. I loathe money so much that I cannot endure the sound, the smell, the touch, or the taste of it! I cannot reveal this to anyone, for they will mock me mercilessly. But because you asked, I am telling you. Money is my greatest fear.'

His guest looked at him with wide-eyed surprise, then nodded and finished his drink.

'I will leave now,' he rose. 'I'll meet you tomorrow

as usual. Good night!'

When his visitor left, Kim sank to the ground, exhausted from having had to restrain himself from shrieking in fear and running far away. But hope flickered inside him, because now he knew what he had to do.

The next day, Kim was very busy. He headed into the village and bargained with one of the farmers for his old cow, which was headed to the slaughterhouse anyway. The farmer was very puzzled, but let Kim take the cow away. Kim then killed the cow himself and carefully collected all its blood in a couple of buckets. As the sun sank below the horizon, Kim knew it was time. He took the buckets out, and splashed the blood all around the house, not leaving even an inch uncovered. He then went inside and stood near the open door, waiting for his visitor.

As the Dokkaebi drew closer to the house, he began to writhe in distress. He could smell the blood, and icy fear made his body cold.

'I thought we were friends!' He shouted at Kim. 'You know I am terrified of blood. What have you done?'

'You weren't honest with me,' Kim yelled back. 'Now I know what you are—you are Dokkaebi. And you want to make me one too. You were never my friend. Now go far away from me, and never, ever come back!'

'I'll be back, just wait and see! I'll never rest till I get my revenge on you!' The Dokkaebi vanished, screaming and shrieking in fear and anger.

Kim slammed the door shut, his breath coming in fast gasps as he collapsed on the floor. He was in real trouble now.

He could barely sleep that night. Visions of the Dokkaebi returning and tearing him into pieces troubled him, and when he woke up, he could barely walk or talk. He remained hidden in his hut, too afraid to even venture out. He drifted in and out of a haze, his heart pounding with fright every time he thought of the Dokkaebi. What would happen to him?

As night fell, Kim trembled with worry. Every little noise startled him, and he could barely keep himself together. Right around the time his guest normally visited, there was a sound of twigs being trampled, as though someone had stepped on them. Kim froze, and closed his eyes. This was it. This was the end. The Dokkaebi would now tear him from limb to limb, and he would die a gory death.

Something crashed against his door, and he jumped into the air.

'You thought I wouldn't be back for my revenge?' The Dokkaebi roared outside, and Kim shrank into the corner of the hut. 'You forgot that I know you just as much as you know me. I will leave this wretched place, but so will you. I hope you die from fright!'

Kim waited, praying to all the Gods he knew, but it was soon silent. He could hear the sounds of insects and the rustling of leaves on the trees, but nothing else. He had to get out of here as soon as he could. He crept to the door and opened it just a crack. All he could see was the inky darkness of the night. The Dokkaebi had truly disappeared.

But what was that on the floor?

Kim opened the door wide, and when he stepped out, he could not believe his eyes! Gold coins lay scattered all across the threshold, winking up at him.

His plan had worked! He had tricked the Dokkaebi into believing that his greatest fear was money!

Laughter erupted out of Kim, as he collapsed on the floor, gathering up the coins and pouring them down again on the floor in disbelief. His plan of using blood to chase the Dokkaebi away had no doubt worked, but his invention of his biggest fear had worked brilliantly as well!

And thus, Kim became the richest man in the village. His appearance returned to normal, and the villagers were all too happy to walk, talk, and work with him. He was a generous man, and the farmer who sold him the cow was astonished by the large reward Kim bestowed on him. The Dokkaebi was never seen around those parts again, and Kim's story of how he outwitted the Dokkaebi was told and retold for many years to come.

# Robin Hood to the Rescue

*Robin Hood is a very well-known figure in English folklore. Together with his band of Merry Men—which includes such figures as Little John and Friar Tuck—and his bag of tricks, he is said to have made life miserable for the very mean Sheriff of Nottingham. He and his band would steal from the rich to help the poor. So, while they were popular with the average citizen, they were hated by royalty. Robin Hood's many adventures remain popular to this day and are even now being made into movies.*

Many years ago, in the country of England, there was a village called Nottingham. The head of this village, or the sheriff as he was called, was a vile man who created nothing but trouble for the villagers. He was arrogant and cruel, and he had his men raid the granaries and the farms to confiscate all the food and meat of the villagers. While the villagers suffered with no food and shivered outside in the cold with no furs to keep them warm, the sheriff and his men feasted inside on rich delicacies and got drunk on the delicious wine. Obviously, the villagers hated the sheriff, but they lived in fear of him, for he was wilful and he could suddenly swoop down on them and arrest an entire family on some flimsy pretext.

In the woods, on the outskirts of Nottingham, lived

the nemesis of the sheriff. He was none other than Robin Hood. He and his band of Merry Men were smart, stealthy, and strong. They often wreaked havoc on the sheriff and his men, stealing food, clothing, and money, and distributing it among poor villagers. Obviously, the villagers loved Robin Hood and, in their eyes, he could never do any r wrong. He was their saviour and prince, and they would give up their lives for him.

One day, as Robin Hood was travelling through the forest, he chanced upon an old woman weeping bitterly.

'Dear lady,' he said softly, as he approached her. 'Dear lady, why are you weeping? What has happened? Do tell me.'

The old woman only beat her chest and wept even more loudly.

'You need to stop crying and tell me exactly what has happened if you want me to help you,' Robin Hood said firmly.

The sobs of the old woman ceased. She wiped her tears and said in a trembling voice, 'My three sons are going to die. And I have no way of saving them. What else do you expect me to do other than cry?'

'Why are they going to die?' Robin Hood raised an eyebrow. 'What do you mean? Speak plainly and be clear.'

The old woman took a deep breath.

'My three sons are going to be hanged today, in the village square. The sheriff had them arrested and dragged away. I have spent the morning on my knees, begging and pleading with the sheriff to show mercy and let them go, but he refused and threw me out.'

'Hanged?' Robin Hood was thoughtful. 'What did

they do? Did they rob a church? Did they kill a priest? Did they manhandle a young lady? What crime did they commit that was so heinous that they are to be hanged?'

The old woman began weeping again.

'They did nothing of that sort, absolutely nothing of that sort. I have taught my sons to be respectful of God and church. Why would they ever rob a church? I have taught my sons to obey the priest. Why would they ever kill him? And I have taught my sons to respect everyone, be they ladies or gentlemen. Why would they manhandle a lady? They have not committed any crimes, believe me. My sons are honourable men, and they would die rather than do anything that would bring dishonour to our family.'

'You have still not answered my question,' Robin Hood said, growing impatient. 'Tell me, what did they do that the sheriff decided that they needed to be hanged?'

The old woman wept some more and wrapped her shawl tighter, pulling at it.

'We had not had a proper meal in a week,' she whispered. 'All our provisions—our grain and meat—had been taken away by the sheriff. We had been living on water and berries and we were starving. My sons saw some deer in the woods, and decided to hunt them. At least that would provide some food. We were desperate, believe me.'

'Did they kill the deer?' Robin asked.

'Yes, they killed the deer. And when they began to skin the deer, the sheriff's men arrived. They caught my sons and thrashed them. They said that the deer belonged to the sheriff and my sons had absolutely no right to hunt them. They said that by killing the deer, my sons had committed a grave crime. They dragged my sons away and the sheriff issued an immediate verdict that they were guilty and deserved nothing less than to be hanged. I begged and pleaded with him, for I have no one but my sons. But the sheriff did not listen and had me thrown out. What could I have done? Stayed and watched my sons take their last breath in the village square? I could not do that, so I came away. And so, here I lie, weeping for my children.'

Robin Hood took a deep breath to control the rage that swept through him. The sheriff was growing more vicious day by day. What could the villagers do if they were left to starve? They broke their backs growing their crops and brewing their drinks. They sold their harvests for a few miserable coins. The sheriff had them at his mercy, confiscating their belongings without a thought, feasting on their hard work without a care, and punishing them cruelly without any fear whatsoever of the consequences. Since he was lord and master, no one dared to question him, much less rebel against him.

'Wipe your tears, dear mother,' Robin Hood said softly, as he knelt beside the lady and took her hands in his. 'I promise you that I will bring your sons back to you, no matter what it costs me.'

The old lady's sobs grew quieter as she met his steady gaze, hardly daring to hope.

'Do you promise to bring my lads home to me?' She whispered, wiping the tears streaming down her cheeks. 'Alive? Or will I have to mourn over their bodies instead?'

'Mother, I promise you I will bring back your sons to you very much alive, and you will rejoice and pull them into your arms joyously. I promise. Take heart, dear mother.'

'My son!' The old woman embraced Robin Hood, a tremulous smile lighting up her face. 'Just the fact that you are promising me something to look forward to is enough. That you care for this old lady and her worries is enough. God bless you, my son, God bless you!'

'Go back home and prepare a feast, dear mother,' Robin Hood said as he rose. 'My men will come by presently and provide you with all you need. Your sons will no doubt be starving after the adventures they have had. What better reward than a feast prepared by their very own mother's hands? Do you trust my words?'

'I trust you with my life, dear son,' said the old woman. 'I will do as you say, and hurry home. I have much work to do.'

Robin Hood waited till she was out of sight before he began walking again towards the village. He was deep in thought for he had to come up with a foolproof plan to rescue the lads. As he strode through the woods, mulling over his options, he came across an old man who was shuffling down the path.

'Good day to you, Sir!' Robin Hood said in a cheerful tone.

'Good day?' the old man grumbled, not looking up. 'Three young men are to be hanged today in the village, and you say "good day"? What is the world coming to? I need a drink! I wish I had money to drown my sorrows in a long cold drink.'

'Is that right?' Robin Hood stared at the old man. 'You are in need of a few coins?'

'I'm no beggar!' The old man huffed. 'Don't you dare!'

'Well, that thought didn't even cross my mind,' said Robin Hood with a smile. 'I was thinking of a trade, you see. I will give you forty silver shillings...'

'Trade?' The old man scoffed. 'Are you pulling my leg? Do I look like I have anything to trade with you, boy? Just move along, nothing to see here. Forty silver shillings, it seems! Pshaw!'

Robin Hood sighed.

'Old man,' he said, blocking his companion's path. 'You do have something to trade. Your clothes. Forget silver, I will give you twenty gold coins for your clothes. What do you say?'

The old man stopped short in utter astonishment.

'My c..clothes?' He stuttered, looking down at himself. 'These rags? You want to pay me in gold for these bits and pieces? Have you gone soft in the head, lad?'

Robin Hood laughed. 'Kind Sir, I am not deluded or mad. I need these clothes urgently. And I am ready to pay for them. You can go ahead and treat yourself to a long cold drink at the village tavern. Do we have a deal?'

'And how will I go to the village tavern? I will be as naked as the day I was born if I give you all my clothes.'

Robin Hood threw back his head and let out a guffaw. 'You certainly know how to bargain, you old thief! You can take my clothes and my money.'

The old man shrugged. 'A fool and his money are

soon parted. Take my clothes, lad. I have a drink waiting for me.'

In a few minutes, the old man was clad in Robin Hood's clothes, and was looking as good as new. He looked at the younger man and sniggered.

'Don't you look fine, dressed in my old rags!' He smirked.

Robin Hood grinned.

'Your clothes are the finest patchwork in the country, I declare!' He said with a flourish. 'The blue, red and yellow patches bring out the dirt on your cloak so well. Your hat has holes in all the right places so that the head will never get sweaty on a hot summer's day. And your shoes are also so fashion-forward. They barely have any soles and are torn enough for my toes to breathe. Of course I look fine—as fashionable as a Lord in the King's Court!'

'That you do, my Lord!' The old man chortled as he jingled the bag of coins Robin Hood had given him. 'Whatever you have up your torn sleeve, I wish you the best of luck! Meanwhile, I shall drink long and hard at the village tavern to your good fortune and success.'

'I will find you tomorrow, when you have passed out and are still asleep there!' Robin Hood teased.

'Fare you well, kind Sir,' the old man bowed and shuffled away. 'Good luck!'

'I shall certainly need all the luck,' Robin Hood muttered, trying not to breathe too deeply. The old man's clothes were as stinky as week-old cabbage soup and were almost making him gag.

He set off at a brisk pace towards the village and soon he reached the sheriff's house. It was right opposite the village square, and the sheriff's men were getting it ready for the hanging that was to happen later that day. The village folk were scurrying away in fear, trying to keep out of the way of these brash and arrogant men, who had no qualms stealing some apples or snatching a jug of milk from the poor people trying to market their wares.

'Who do we have here?' One of the guards sneered at Robin Hood, looking at him up and down in disdain.

'I want to speak to the sheriff,' Robin Hood said, disguising his voice and hunching over like an old man.

'Oh! And I would like to seek an audience with the King!' The guard mocked, and the other guards laughed loudly.

'I heard there was going to be a hanging,' muttered Robin Hood.

'Yeah, yeah, you can watch the circus later when it happens. The sheriff is not handing out special invitations!'

'What's going on?' The sheriff's voice interrupted the guards who were huddling around Robin Hood, itching to taunt and bully him.

'This old man wants to speak to you, Sire,' the first guard said, and pushed Robin Hood with his staff. 'We were just trying to find out what he wanted.'

'Is that right?' The sheriff stepped forward and studied Robin Hood in disgust. 'What do you want from me, you beggar?'

'Well, I heard there was a hanging, and I've been a hangman before. So, I was looking for some work and someone told me to come and ask the sheriff,' Robin Hood mumbled.

'You've been a hangman before?' The sheriff's eyebrows rose.

Robin Hood nodded.

'Well, well, isn't that just perfect?' The sheriff laughed. 'My hangman ran away because he felt I was hanging too many folks—the useless chap! You've come to the right place, my man.'

He clapped Robin Hood on the shoulder.

'So, what's your fee? Do you want a meal? Or shall I give you some old clothes so that you can throw these awful rags away? I'm not giving you any money, let's be clear about that.'

'Oh, I don't want any money, Sire,' Robin Hood said in an earnest voice. 'No food, no clothes, none of that. But I do have a request. If you would oblige me, I would be most grateful.'

'A request?' The sheriff shook his head. 'Come, come, you are not going to ask me to set these lads free, are you? Unless you're ready to take their place, I would think twice about such requests.'

'Oh no, no, no, Sire!' Robin Hood fell to his knees as if pleading. 'I would never, ever think of showing you such disrespect. Never. All I have is a humble and simple request. Other villages forbade me from doing this. It is just a fascination of mine.'

The sheriff shrugged.

'What is it? Come on, tell me quick. I don't have all day to sit and listen to your tall tales, old man!'

Robin Hood put his hand under his cloak and brought out a horn.

'This is my horn, Sire. It is loud and it is sharp. And all I want to do is to blow on it three times just before the hanging, so that everyone in the village knows what is about to happen.'

'You want to blow a horn? Three times? Just before the hanging? That's it?' The sheriff looked at Robin Hood in disbelief, as the latter nodded in agreement.

'If I agree to this foolish request of yours, I would not be bound to give you anything else as a fee, right? I would neither give you food nor drink, nor any old clothes, nor any coin. Are we agreed?'

'Absolutely, Sire!' Robin Hood bowed low and the sheriff shook his head and rolled his eyes. 'Very well, it is agreed.'

A hush fell over the village as the sun began its descent into the western sky. The three frightened lads were brought out to the platform. They stood there with their heads bowed, hiding their tear-stained cheeks, their hands bound behind their backs. The villagers were all safe in their homes. They peered through peepholes, through their curtains, and through cracks in the walls, cowering in fright as the sheriff's men stomped about, looking mean and vicious.

'Where's the hangman?' The sheriff shouted. 'Get him here. Don't waste my time!'

Robin Hood shuffled to the platform.

'I am here, Sire, and ready. Can I get my fee now?'

'Yeah, yeah, go on, blow your stupid horn!' The sheriff answered, rolling his eyes.

Suddenly the old man stood up straighter than it looked possible for him. He placed the horn to his mouth and blew three times. The three sharp blasts echoed through the land, loud and clear as if sounding a warning.

'What's that?' The sheriff's men looked at each other as they heard a roaring sound in the distance, which was drawing closer every minute. 'What's that?' They asked each other in fear and horror, moving closer to each other, their hands hovering on their weapons.

A loud shout was heard and suddenly the village square swarmed with fierce looking men. Their bows were drawn, with their arrows all aimed straight at the sheriff and his men.

'What on earth...?' The sheriff looked astounded as the old man threw off his cloak.

'R... Robin Hood? You...you...' The sheriff spluttered, red with indignation.

'Yes, indeed, Robin Hood at your service,' Robin Hood smiled at the sheriff, then turned to his men. 'Thank you very much indeed for agreeing to my request. How else could I have signalled to my men?'

He turned to his men, and barked out orders to free the three young lads.

'Your mother awaits you. She has prepared a feast for you and you will be the feast for her eyes,' Robin Hood said, as the three young men wept with joy and thanked him gratefully.

'Take them to their mother,' Robin Hood ordered his men.

Before the sheriff and his men could realize what was happening, Robin Hood and his men had completely vanished from the scene.

The old woman could not believe her eyes when she saw her sons returning home, safe and sound.

'Thank you, Robin Hood!' She said, wiping tears of joy from her eyes. 'You kept your word.'

'I always keep my promises!' Robin Hood said to her and smiled, as he and his men sat down to feast and celebrate.

# Naughty Loki

*Of late, Loki has become very well known as a member of the Marvel universe. But even prior to that, Loki was a known name. He is a god from Norse mythology who has often been portrayed as a companion to the gods Odin and Thor. Odin, the ruler of Asgard, is known as the Allfather and is wise and knowledgeable. Thor, his son, the mighty god of thunder, symbolizes strength and courage. Together, they reflect the Norse belief that both wisdom and strength are equally important. Loki has shape-shifting abilities. He is a perpetual trickster who enjoys creating mischief and playing pranks, and manages to embarrass the gods on a regular basis. But he is also very smart and often comes up with solutions to tricky situations. There are many interesting stories about him and he is also sometimes referred to as the God of Fire.*

Loki was bored. Nothing interesting or fun was happening in the heavens. Freya, the goddess of love and beauty, was napping after a lavish lunch, Odin was dozing off, and Thor was out challenging his friends to a show of strength (as usual, the show-off!).

Loki wandered into Thor's living quarters and came upon Sif, Thor's wife, who was fast asleep on the couch. Her gorgeous blonde hair spilled over the back of the couch and fell in cascades to the ground.

She was envied for her beautiful hair all around the world, and Thor loved to run his fingers through her silky locks.

As always, Loki was in a mischievous mood.

'Well, well, well, what do we have here?' He mused softly, as he stood at the foot of the couch.

'I think a change of scene would do everyone good,' he said with a naughty grin and produced a pair of fine sharp scissors. In a trice, he had chopped off all of Sif's hair, and the golden tresses lay on the floor like a carpet.

Just at that moment, Thor walked in, all sweaty and thirsty from the wrestling match he had just competed in.

'What are you doing here, Loki?' He asked, frowning. He knew Loki could never be up to any good, so he wasn't pleased to see him in his house.

'Er...nothing really,' Loki said, quickly hiding the scissors behind his back. 'Just strolling around, seeing if anything interesting is happening.'

Thor took a swig of the cold water that stood in a jug on the table, and wiped his mouth.

'Is that right? I can see Sifis having a nice nap. I hope you have not been disturbing her.' Thor said, drinking some more water to quench his thirst.

'Oh no, no, not at all,' Loki said, raising his hands. He immediately realized his mistake. Thor glared at the scissors in his hand and advanced threateningly towards him.

'Loki,' he growled, 'what are you doing with those scissors?'

His feet touched the luxuriant hair and he looked

down. As realization dawned on him, Thor's face grew dark with fury.

'What have you done?' He snarled, startling Sif, who woke up with a start.

'What's happening?' she said, brushing her hair and starting with shock when her fingers reached the jagged tips.

'My hair!' She wailed.

'LOKI!' Thor roared. Loki turned to run, but Thor had already caught him and had him firmly within his grip. 'How dare you?'

Sif was sobbing, sitting down among the whorls of hair that lay lifeless on the ground.

'All right, all right, I am sorry,' Loki said, looking a little ashamed. 'I did it on a whim. I was bored...'

'Seriously?' Thor tightened his hold, glowering at him. 'You cut off my wife's hair on a whim? Did you think I would let you get away with it? I am going to kill you!'

'I'm sorry, I'm sorry!' Loki yelled. 'You know me. I can't help myself.'

'I can't help myself either,' Thor shouted. 'I am going to kill you right now.'

'Wait, Thor,' Sif intervened, still sobbing. 'He said he's sorry. Don't threaten him like this, please.'

'Yes, Thor,' Loki said, 'listen to your wife. She is more sensible than you.'

'You need to keep quiet, else you will regret it,' Thor glared at him.

'Leave him, Thor,' Sif said, wiping her tears. 'Even if you kill him, it's not like I am going to get my hair back.' A fresh burst of sobs made her turn away.

Loki now felt really bad for what he had done.

'OK, listen,' he told Thor. 'I am really very, very sorry. I should not have done this. I will make it up to you.'

'Really? And how do you plan on doing that?' Thor raised an eyebrow, loosening his hold a little.

'I will go to the sons of Ivaldi, and beg them to make Sif a beautiful wig,' Loki said. 'I don't care what they ask for in return, I will give them everything I have, even my life if I have to. But I will get Sif her beautiful hair back. Believe me, Thor. I give you my word.'

The sons of Ivaldi were a group of dwarves renowned for their craftsmanship. Their creations were unbelievably wondrous. If anyone could restore Sif's hair, it was definitely them. If Loki was going to enlist them, then perhaps there was some room for forgiveness after all.

Thor released Loki reluctantly.

'You had better do as you have said,' Thor wagged a finger at the mischievous god. 'The next time I see you, I want to see you with Sif's hair. Else, don't bother showing your face around here, unless you want to turn up very dead.'

'I will, I promise,' Loki said. 'Sif, please don't cry, I beg you. I have promised and I will keep my word. The next time you see me, I will be here with your beautiful hair.'

Sif hugged him and bade him safe passage to Svartalfheim, the land of the Black Elves. Legend has it that Svartalfheim was formed from the primordial void from which the world itself had begun. The dwarves of Svartalfheim were created from the earth itself, drawing from it their superlative creativity and power. It was the home of the greatest craftsmen ever, and was filled with the clang of hammers, the heat of the hearth, and the roar of the bellows. It was located deep within the earth and the journey was perilous. The rugged terrain made the going difficult, the maze of caves and tunnels were confusing and disorienting, and worst of all, the shadows that danced between the glimmers of light proved to be very unsettling. But Loki persevered and soon reached Svartalfheim.

Loki sought out the sons of Ivaldi, who had the reputation of being the best of the best. Loki spent some time describing what he needed, and they agreed to make it for him. Who hadn't heard of Sif's lustrous long hair! Stories of her beauty had managed to travel to the interiors of the earth, the land of the Black Elves. As Loki wandered around the place, he was impressed with the superior artisanship of the craftsmen, and the wondrous items they made.

When it was time, he went back to the sons of Ivaldi. He was amazed by what they had accomplished. The long golden silken tresses they presented were not just a match, but an improvement on Sif's original hair! Apart from that, since he was, after all, a god, they also had for him two other marvels as presents. One was a ship called Skidbladnir. This was a marvellous feat of engineering indeed because the ship could be folded down to a size small enough to fit inside a pocket. It would also catch the wind no matter when its sail was raised. If this was a fantastic present, the second was even more so: Gungnir, a magical spear that could not be stopped once released.

Loki was indeed very impressed with the gifts, and thanked the sons of Ivaldi profusely.

If he had been any other god, Loki would have returned straight to the heavens and given the gifts to Sif and the other gods. And that would have been the end of the story. However, he was truly the god of mischief and he couldn't resist getting into more trouble.

He strolled over to the dwarf brothers Brokkr and Sindri. They were master craftsmen in their own right and they were very busy indeed, making all sorts of marvellous things. Brokkr worked the bellows unceasingly and Sindri poured and fashioned the metal. Both of them were drenched in perspiration, yet their focus was completely and unwaveringly on their work. They were deserving of every bit of their fame. Of course, Loki decided to stir things up.

'Hello, hello! Greetings from the heavens,' he hollered at the dwarf brothers, who nodded their greetings and continued their work.

'They told me that you two are the best of the best, so I had to come and see for myself. You are no doubt impressive but...'

Sindri and Brokkr glanced at each other, their brows furrowing in query. What was Loki implying? That they were not impressive?

Loki shrugged. 'From what I can see, you doubtless do a fine job but...'

'All right!' Brokkr put down his bellows and put his hands on his hips. 'Just what are you trying to say, Loki? Out with it. We don't have time to stand around waiting for pearls of wisdom to drop from your lips.'

'Er...,' Loki looked around as if checking whether

someone was spying on them or not, and his voice dropped into a conspiratorial whisper. 'I'm not saying you are not good, but rumour has it that the sons of Ivaldi are far, far superior to you.'

Sindri marched up to Loki with an angry glare, and almost poked him in the eye.

'Who said that? Tell me, who had the gall to say that someone is superior to us?'

'I don't want to cause any trouble,' Loki lied, a grin hovering around his lips. 'But look, these are what the sons of Ivaldi made for me to take to the heavens as gifts for the gods. Look at this wondrous ship! And look at this fantastic spear! Honestly, I won't be surprised if you cannot surpass this.'

'In fact,' Loki pursed his lips and tapped a finger on his chin, 'I am so sure that you cannot ever surpass this that I am willing to bet my very head on it! What do you say?'

Brokkr and Sindri stared at him in disbelief, and then burst out laughing. They laughed till tears rolled down their cheeks, and they held their aching sides and stomachs as they tried to stop laughing in vain.

'Hahaha! Hahaha!' Sindri laughed breathlessly. 'Did you just hear what he said?'

'He bet his own head! Hahaha! Hahaha!' Brokkr guffawed, and it set them off again.

'Will you stop laughing?' Loki said crossly. 'You both look like clowns, rolling on the floor like that.'

'You started it!' Brokkr said. The dwarf brothers laughed and laughed till they collapsed quite exhausted on the floor.

Once they had recovered, Brokkr and Sindri got down to serious business.

'We are going to prove to you that we are the best of the best,' they announced. 'Just wait till you see the gifts that we make for the gods, and you will lose your head for sure, in more than one way!'

Sindri and Brokkr began to work in earnest, and Loki soon realized that he was undoubtedly going to lose his bet. That did not put him in a good mood at all. He could not imagine having to lose his head over such a silly bet. But the dwarf brothers were taking this all too seriously and they would no doubt demand his head in return. He had to do something to make their work suffer.

'Oh bother!' Brokkr said, agitated. 'This fly is buzzing around and annoying me so much!'

'Watch the bellows, brother,' Sindri called. 'We can't afford to make any mistakes.'

Brokkr tried hard to keep working the bellows despite the fly. But just at the right moment, Loki, who had turned himself into a fly, bit him hard on his hands.

'Ouch!' Brokkr shook his hand. 'I'm going to kill this fly! Sorry Sindri, did I stop the bellows at the wrong time?'

'Not at all!' said Sindri, holding up his creation proudly. 'Behold Gullinbursti!'

'That is beautiful!' Brokkr exclaimed. It was indeed a wondrous thing they had both fashioned—a boar that had a lustrous gold mane and glowed in the dark.

'It can run on both water and air, faster than even horses!' Sindri told Loki, who smiled and nodded, concealing his worry.

'Marvellous!' He praised. 'But, you've taken so much time to make just one gift,' he added, to needle the brothers. 'I think the sons of Ivaldi were faster.'

Brokkr scowled. 'We can do better, just you wait,' he said, and the brothers returned to work.

Once again, Loki transformed himself into a fly and buzzed around.

'Grrrr! This aggravating fly again!' Brokkr shouted. 'Sindri, just kill it, won't you?'

'I can't suddenly stop pouring out molten gold,' Sindri scolded. 'And you had better not stop working the bellows even for a minute, otherwise all the work we've done so far will just have gone down the drain, and Loki will have won the bet. You don't want that, do you?'

Brokkr grumbled but focused on the bellows. Again, just at the crucial moment, Loki bit Brokkr's neck.

'Ouch!' Brokkr swatted the fly away. 'This irritating fly is driving me crazy! Oops! Did I stop the bellows at the wrong time, Sindri?'

'No, you just missed it by a second, thank God!' His brother replied. 'Just look at what we've made! Lo and behold—Draupnir!'

'That is indeed a grand ring,' Loki agreed.

'It is not just a grand ring, it is magical too,' said Sindri proudly. 'It will sprout eight identical rings every ninth night. Can the sons of Ivaldi do this?'

Loki rolled his eyes.

'Well, if I had given them as much time as I have given you, perhaps they would have come up with something even better!'

'Not a chance!' Brokkr barked. 'Brother, let us prove

to this doubting god once and for all that we are the best indeed.'

They went back to work ferociously, for they were determined to win the bet. Loki was most anxious, for it certainly looked like they would win the bet and he would lose his head. This was his last chance to defeat them.

Once again, he turned himself into a fly and waited for the opportune moment.

Sindri was completely absorbed in his work. Brokkr worked the bellows unceasingly. Loki could tell that the brothers were determined to do a brilliant job, but he was equally determined to ensure that they did not win the bet.

'Almost done,' shouted Sindri. 'Don't stop even for a moment, my brother.'

Brokkr nodded, his muscles bulging under the strain of working the bellows with vigour. Sweat dripped from his forehead, but he did not pause to wipe it. This was exactly the moment Loki was waiting for.

'Aaaaargh!' Brokkr screamed in pain as he let go of the bellows and put his hands on his eyes.

'BROKKR!' Sindri roared. 'I told you not to stop even for a moment!'

'But the damned fly bit my eye!' Brokkr protested, even as he resumed pumping the bellows. Blood streamed from his eye, but he dared not disobey his brother.

'Well, well, well,' Loki chuckled, quickly having transformed himself back into his usual shape. 'What do we have here? Has an unfortunate accident damaged the goods?'

'You wish!' Sindri barked at him. 'Look at what we have wrought—this most wondrous hammer, the Mjölnir!'

'But the handle looks a bit short, doesn't it?' Brokkr whispered to his brother, who nudged at him to keep quiet.

'And pray tell—what does this wondrous hammer do?' Loki said, looking uninterested.

'Only someone worthy enough to wield it will find out,' replied Sindri. 'Now it is time. Brokkr my brother, it would be best if you accompanied Loki with the gifts, and let the gods decide who are the better craftsmen.'

'As you wish, brother,' Brokkr said, and collected all the three awesome treasures that they had crafted.

'Watch out for Loki and his mischief,' Sindri whispered. 'I do not trust him, and I am sure he will try to wriggle out of the bet one way or another because I know in my heart of hearts that we are the best craftsmen in the world! Good luck, my brother!'

When Loki and Brokkr reached their destination, the gods were very impressed with all the gifts.

'To you, my dear Sif, I present these lustrous locks along with my sincerest apologies for having caused you such distress in the first place,' Loki bowed to Sif, who accepted his gift with delight. Thor beamed as his wife snapped her wig into place—she was surely the most beautiful woman in the world!

'To you Odin, I give Gungnir, so that you can find your mark wherever it may be.' Odin looked very pleased with the spear indeed.

'Freya, to you I present the Skidbladnirmay you travel far and wide.'

'These are marvellous indeed!' Sif gushed.

'Yes, these have been crafted by the sons of Ivaldi, the best craftsmen in the world,' Loki declared with a flourish.

This prompted Brokkr to come forward. He frowned at a smirking Loki before he bowed to the gods before him.

'Sindri and I are most honoured to present to you the gifts we crafted with our own hands,' Brokkr announced.

'My Lady,' he bowed to Freya, 'we are indeed proud to present our splendid creation, the boar that glows in the dark, and can run through both water and air faster than even horses. May your hunts be successful forever.'

'This is really a very clever and wondrous creation, Brokkr,' Freya said with a big smile that showed how delighted she was. 'I am very pleased indeed.'

'Oh please!' Loki scoffed. 'I've seen better things.'

Brokkr ignored him and turned to Odin.

'My Lord,' he bowed. 'We are also very happy to present to you this magical ring, from which will spring forth eight magical rings every ninth night. You will never run short of magic in your life.'

'Magnificent!' Odin beamed. 'I am truly pleased with your amazing gift.'

'Really?' Loki mocked. 'A Ring? You're happy with a ring?'

'A magic ring, Loki!' Odin laughed at him. 'Don't look so put out.'

Brokkr had saved the best for the last.

'My Lord,' he bowed to Thor. 'For you, we have

brought this specially crafted fabulous hammer. It will come right back to you every time you throw it.'

Thor hefted the hammer in his hands and whirled it around.

'The handle is a trifle short, isn't it?' He asked, and Loki hid his grin.

'The handle is perfectly designed to work with your magnificent body, My Lord,' Brokkr bowed again, cursing the fly that had wrought the damage. 'Just try it and see.'

Thor shrugged, then hurled the hammer at a jug. The hammer flew into the air, hit its target perfectly, smashing the jug to smithereens, and then flew right back into Thor's waiting hand.

'This is superb!' Thor looked as excited as a child who's been given a new toy. 'This hammer has indeed been perfectly designed for me. How awesome is that!'

Loki began to edge away from the group.

'Now that you have seen all the gifts, my lords and ladies,' Brokkr said, 'I have a kind request. See, Loki and we have a little bet going as to who are the better craftsmen—the sons of Ivaldi, or Sindri and myself. I would be much obliged if the gods themselves would pronounce the verdict, having seen the proof of each party's mastery.'

'You see,' Brokkr paused dramatically, and pointed to Loki just as he was trying to disappear from the room. 'Loki has said he is willing to bet his head that the sons of Ivaldi are better than us.'

'Is that right?' Thor stared at Loki. 'Is this true, Loki? Did you bet your head?'

'Umm, yes, I did,' Loki said shame-facedly.

'Well, unfortunately for you, I agree with Brokkr that he and Sindri are the better craftsmen,' Thor said, sitting back and crossing his arms.

'I agree,' Odin said, and Freya and Sif nodded their agreement.

'So, I get your head!' Brokkr said, a gleam in his eyes as he advanced towards Loki, tugging at the knife tucked into his waist.

'Not so fast, not so fast,' Loki smiled. 'I agreed that you would get my head, but I said nothing about my neck now, did I?'

'What?' Brokkr stopped short in confusion. 'How else will I get your head?'

'That's up to you to figure out, my dear Brokkr,' Loki laughed. 'You can take my head if you can leave my neck out of it.'

'But that's impossible!' Brokkr argued. He turned to the gods in despair. 'This isn't fair. He was the one who placed the bet, and he was the one who wagered his head. We won the bet fair and square—you gods are witness to this.'

The gods smiled.

'Never underestimate Loki, my dear fellow,' Thor said. 'He is not called the god of mischief for nothing. What he says is true though. Either you figure out a way to get his head without his neck, or you let him go.'

Brokkr's shoulders drooped in defeat.

'Well, I surrender. He is too clever for me. I have no way of doing that. So, he is free of the wager.'

'We will still find a way of punishing you, Loki,'

Thor called after the figure that danced out of the room, laughing in glee.

'Good luck with that!' Loki laughed and disappeared, no doubt to wreak havoc somewhere else in the universe.

# Clever Kitty

*Puss in Boots is a folktale from Italy, about how a cat helps his master become rich and even win the hand of a princess in marriage. It became hugely popular when Charles Perrault included it in his collection of fairy tales. Puss in Boots has inspired popular culture greatly, and has been included in several artistic productions. Puss in Boots even features as a character in the movie* Shrek. *Here we offer a slightly modified version of the tale—let's see if you can spot what is different.*

The miller's house was in mourning for he had passed away. People came from far and wide to pay their respects since the miller had been a good man. His three sons stood with their heads bowed as folks filed past, sharing their condolences on this terrible loss. Finally, everyone left, and the house was silent.

'It is time to read Papa's will,' said the eldest son, and he took out a scroll of paper from his waist.

'In the event of my passing away, this is what I bequeath to my three sons. To my first son, I give my mill. May he always work hard and become prosperous. To my second son, I give my donkey. May he travel far and become rich. To my youngest son, I give my cat. May she always be his friend and benefactor.'

The eldest son rolled up the scroll, exchanged

glances with the middle brother, and they both burst out laughing.

'A cat as a friend and benefactor!' The second brother chortled. 'Never thought that Father could pull off such a good joke!'

The youngest son's face drooped. He had always thought he had been his father's favourite son. Why had he just left his cat to him then? Was he not worthy of anything else? He had been kind and gentle and patient, always giving of himself to others in need. Surely his father did not leave just his cat to him?

But he pulled himself together. He knew that his father had loved the cat very much. He would definitely do his best to take good care of the pet. That was the least that he could do.

Leaving his brothers to celebrate their good fortune, the boy went to the barn.

'Here Kitty, Kitty!' He called out, hoping to lure the cat out.

A beautiful white cat strolled out of the barn, her eyes watchful and her tail alert.

'There you are,' said the lad. 'Father has left you in my care. Come on, let me give you some milk.'

The cat followed him to the kitchen, then jumped on the table and lapped up the saucer of milk he had placed there. When she was finished, she sat licking her body with long strokes of her tongue. The boy stroked her head gently.

'What am I supposed to do, Puss?' He asked. 'Father has left me nothing, except for you. It won't be long before my brothers kick me out of the house. How will I make a living? Forget about feeding and clothing myself, how will I look after you?'

'You don't need to worry about that, Master.'

The lad whirled around at the sound of the soft voice. There was no one else in the kitchen, so who was speaking?

'Master, it is I,' Puss sat up and said, looking the boy straight in the eye.

'You? B...but you're a c...cat!' The young boy spluttered in astonishment. 'You can talk? You are a talking cat? Dear Lord!'

Puss rolled her eyes and sighed.

*'Yes, yes, I am a talking cat. I am your very own miracle. Now listen to me, and listen carefully. Your father made me promise I would be your friend and benefactor. And I hold that promise sacred. Do not worry, I will take care of you, and I will win you your fortune.'*

'My fortune?' The boy squeaked. 'But you're a *cat*!'

Puss sighed again. This boy was quite slow. He would need all the help she could possibly give him.

'Yes, I think we have established that I am a talking cat, that you are my master, and that I will take care of you,' she said.

'Take care of me? How?' The boy raised his eyebrows so high that they almost disappeared into his hair.

'I will share my plans with you on a need-to-know basis,' Puss said, her nose up in the air. 'And right now, you don't need to know.'

'Of course you have *plans*!' The boy huffed. 'And what might they be, these lofty plans that you have? Oh, let me see. Perhaps you will have me challenge the child-eating ogre, who is on a rampage in the countryside, to a duel, and kill him? Perhaps that will impress the king so much that he will offer me the hand of the princess? And then we will all live happily ever after?'

'Well boy, I must admit, you have completely impressed me! You've cracked it; you've hit the nail on the head and guessed all my wicked plans!' Puss smirked and the boy glared at her.

'Are you done, your highness?' He scowled. 'I need to go and sit and think about our future, and make *actual* plans so that we don't starve to death.'

'I'm not done!' Puss drew herself up and stared at him till he blinked. 'I promised your father I would take care of you, and I never, ever break my promise. So, listen up. I need you to do something for me. Go and get me some boots and a bag. Right now! Hurry!'

'All right, all right!' The boy scrambled to his feet. 'No need to get all worked up. Boots and a bag—got it. And I am supposed to be the master...!' he grumbled, as he walked out of the kitchen.

Puss curled up and closed her eyes with a grin. Master indeed. Ha!

The boy walked to the shoemaker and ordered the finest boots for his cat. He couldn't afford to pay the shoemaker, so he did all the chores in the shop. He cleaned the place, polished the shoes, and made the shoemaker some excellent coffee. When the shoes were ready, the boy picked up a big bag that the shoemaker had generously offered him and put the shoes in it.

'Why on earth would a cat need boots and a bag?' He pondered as he made his way home. 'But then Puss is no ordinary cat, I must remember. I wonder what she wants to do with all this? Perhaps we will set off on an adventure?'

Puss was curled up on a warm stone bench in the sunlight when she was woken by the boy.

'Here you go,' he said, handing the bag to her. 'Your boots and your bag. All set, madam.'

'Excellent!' Puss purred. 'Now off you go and relax, and leave me to my work.'

'This is confusing,' the boy muttered as he walked away. 'I'm the one who's supposed to work, and Puss ought to relax. I'll just take a nap and hopefully, when I wake up, things will not be so topsy-turvy.'

Puss put on the boots and admired herself for a moment. They were excellent shoes indeed, and they fit beautifully and were very comfortable.

'Not bad at following orders, that boy,' she mused as she strolled into the kitchen. She picked out some fresh green lettuce, some crispy orange carrots and a tasty bunch of parsley, then put them all into the bag, slung the bag over her back, and set off. She made her way to the forest at the edge of the property, for she knew there was a really large rabbit warren there, teeming with delicious rabbits.

She placed the lettuce, carrots and parsley in strategic positions and then curled herself into a tight circle and waited. She knew she had to be really patient and she was prepared. Very soon, rabbits popped out of the warren, noses twitching, mouths drooling at the scent and sight of such scrumptious fare. When they emerged, eager to feast on the vegetables, they walked straight into the bag that Puss held. Without a moment's delay, Puss pulled the strings tight to close the mouth of the bag.

'Well, there's your dinner, Master,' she said when she reached home, and laid the bag at his feet.

The boy could hardly believe his eyes.

'You are astonishing!' He cried. 'Who would believe that a cat could indeed take care of a human? Thank you for providing me with enough food to last me a good week. Thank you, dear Puss!'

He attempted to drop a kiss on her head, but she slipped out of his grasp.

'Just a thanks will do fine,' she snarled. 'No need to get all huggy and kissy.'

The boy laughed. 'Thank you, Madam,' he bowed. 'Thank you very much indeed.'

The next day, Puss repeated the same thing. You would think that the rabbits would be a little more wary after the events of the previous day, but they were obsessed with devouring the vegetables. It was too late for them to escape when Puss pulled the strings of the bag to tightly close it once again.

This time however, she did not go to the boy. She headed straight to the palace instead.

'I seek an audience with the king,' she told the guard. 'My master sends a very valuable gift and I must give it to the king himself.'

'Very well,' said the guard. 'Wait here till you are summoned.'

Before long, Puss was admitted into the king's court. The king sat on his throne, rather gloomy and fed up with all the routine matters of his kingdom. He was tired and hungry, and he was dying to eat something different and tasty.

Puss entered the court and bowed low.

'Your Highness,' she purred. 'My master, the Marquis of Carrabas, sends you this present with his respects. We sincerely hope you will enjoy it.'

'What is it?' The king grumbled. His beautiful daughter, who was also in the court with him, took the bag from Puss and peeped inside.

'Oh Father!' She cried in delight. 'The Marquis has sent us a rabbit. Now you can have the rabbit stew you have been craving.'

'Excellent!' The king's face brightened. 'Please tell the Marquis that we are indeed very pleased with his gift.'

I will, your Majesty,' Puss bowed again and prepared to leave.

'Dear Cat,' the princess called out. 'Please come with me for a moment?'

Puss padded behind the princess who took her straight to the kitchen and poured out a large cup of the creamiest cream into it.

'Here you go, Puss,' she said with a smile. 'My father really loves any dish made of rabbit, and can eat them for days on end, so you have made my father very happy indeed. I can't let you go without a reward, can I?'

Puss licked her lips, and without hesitation, lapped up the entire cup of heavenly cream.

'I will be back again tomorrow,' she promised the Princess and took her leave. True to her word, Puss returned every day with rabbit in her bag, with best regards from the Marquis of Carrabas.

Now, it was time for the second step of her plan to be executed.

The next morning, Puss strolled over to a huge, grand castle. No one dared wander near the place because it belonged to the terrible ogre. Puss was not afraid. In fact, she knew that if she played her cards right, she would have the ogre right where she wanted him.

'Oh Ogre!' She called out. 'Look who's come to visit you.'

The ogre emerged from the castle with a frown.

'I have a visitor?' He asked, and his deep scary voice echoed through the castle.

Puss suppressed a shiver.

'Dear Ogre, I know how everyone flees from the very sight or sound of you. They are all so afraid of you. You must be so lonely. Everyone needs a friend or two, don't you think?'

'A friend?' The scowl on the ogre's face deepened.

'Yes, a friend,' Puss purred. 'You know, someone to hang out with—someone to talk to and eat with—and generally have fun?'

'Hmmm,' the ogre thought to himself. 'You're right, I don't have any friends. No one ever comes to my home or offers to spend time with me. Everyone runs away at the very mention of me.'

'That's exactly what I'm saying,' said Puss, drawing closer to the ogre. 'I know how that feels. It must make you so sad.'

'Well, yes, it does make me a bit sad,' the ogre conceded.

'From today, you can consider me as your good friend. I won't ask much of you. I will just spend some time with you and we can talk. I am sure you have lots to talk about.'

The ogre was pleased with Puss. He offered her some food or milk, but Puss declined.

'Tell me all about your adventures,' Puss said, settling down in front of the gigantic fireplace. 'I am sure you will have the most interesting tales to share.'

'Ah yes!' The ogre reclined in his huge wooden chair and began to tell one horrific tale after another. Puss swallowed and shivered, but she kept a straight face and listened to him with her full attention. After a while, she interrupted him.

'So, you mean to tell me that you can actually change into whatever creature you wish? I don't believe it! That's just too preposterous.'

The ogre bristled with indignation. 'You don't believe me? I can show you right now!'

In an instant, he transformed into a roaring lion who jumped in front of Puss. She was so afraid that her whiskers quivered and turned cold at the ends. However, she put on a brave face and yawned.

'All right, all right, I believe you,' she said dismissively. 'It must be easy to turn into such a large and fierce creature. But I doubt very much that you can transform into a small timid creature, say, a mouse?'

'Ha ha!' The ogre chortled. 'You think that's a challenge? Just watch me!'

The next minute, he had transformed into a little grey mouse. Puss had been waiting all along for just this moment. She pounced on him and killed him almost instantly.

'Challenge well met, dear ogre,' she purred. 'Good bye, and thank you!'

Puss rushed back to her master for it was almost time for the king to step out for his daily ride.

'Master! Master!' she mewled. 'Come on quick. I

need you to have a bath in the river at once.'

'What?' The lad had been helping his eldest brother in the mill by carrying sacks of grain and flour. He was covered with fine white powder and looked a complete mess.

If you trust me, you need to come with me to the river right now and have a bath,' Puss commanded. 'I have plans for you.'

'All right, all right,' the boy rolled his eyes. 'So bossy you are. I will do as you command, your Majesty.'

When he reached the river, he stripped off his clothes and left them on the bank before diving into the cool water.

'Puss certainly has the best ideas,' he thought, as he swam lazily in the refreshing waters.

Puss certainly had ideas. She made off with his shabby torn clothes, threw them into a pit, and covered the pit with leaves so that there was no way they could be seen. She did this as fast as she could because she could hear the wheels of the king's chariot approaching. She hurried to the path and stood in the middle, yowling.

The king's chariot drew to an abrupt halt.

'What's going on?' The king grumbled, as he stuck his head out of the window. His eyes widened with surprise when he saw Puss.

'What are you doing here?' He asked. 'Is there a problem? Can I do anything to help you?'

'My master is in trouble!' Puss gasped. 'He went swimming in the river on a whim, and someone has stolen his clothes. When he gets out, he will be so cold that he will freeze to death. Please help, I beg you, please help!'

'For someone who has been sending me gifts every day, I am only too glad to do something in return to help. Soldier, go at once to the palace and fetch a set of my clothes. Hurry, be quick, or I'll have you beheaded!' The king ordered.

Very soon, a new set of handsome clothes were provided, and Puss took them to the miller's son. He was surprised to see the new clothes, but Puss was in a hurry and didn't answer any of his questions.

'Come, come,' she said. 'Someone is waiting for you.'

The miller's son was astonished to see the king waiting for him in his chariot.

'Your Highness!' he bowed low. 'I am speechless. I would never have imagined that I would be meeting you here of all the places.'

'That's fine,' dismissed the king. 'Now get in and I'll drop you home.'

'To my house?' The young man stammered, looking at Puss helplessly. 'Your Highness...'

'He is very grateful for your help,' Puss interrupted, giving her master a glare. 'He will remain indebted to you forever. I will sit in front and show the way to his abode.'

She pushed her master towards the carriage, and he nervously got in. The king gave him a big smile.

As they wound their way through the countryside, the king could not help admiring his surroundings. There were beautiful vineyards, lush with ripe grapes, gorgeous meadows with pretty flowers, and sprawling fields laden with crops bursting with goodness. Every now and then, he would stop the carriage to speak to the locals who were tending the grounds.

'And who does all this belong to?' The king asked repeatedly.

'To the Marquis of Carrabas,' was always the reply. Puss had prepared well, having threatened the locals with dire consequences if they gave any other answer.

'I am impressed,' said the king, looking appreciatively at the miller's son, who just kept smiling and nodding, for he had no clue as to what Puss was planning to pull off.

Soon they pulled up at the ogre's grand castle, for this is where Puss had brought them.

'Welcome to my master's humble abode, Your Majesty,' Puss said with a bow. She nudged her master, who also bowed and mumbled a welcome.

The castle was indeed beautiful, filled with invaluable tapestries, carpets, chandeliers and paintings. The king was truly impressed.

'Since you have come all this way, you must dine with us,' said Puss, and gave her master another nudge.

'Yes, yes, I insist,' said the lad.

'All arrangements have been made. Please come this way,' said Puss.

The king was led into a huge hall, in which there stood a giant table groaning under the most delicious food and drink. The king and his men feasted till their stomachs threatened to burst.

'You are a most impressive young man,' the king said to the miller's son. 'I think you are worthy of my daughter's hand. Will you be gracious enough to marry the princess?'

The lad's jaw fell and he almost choked in astonishment.

'He would be very honoured to accept your proposal, Your Majesty,' Puss intervened quickly. 'Just set the date, and I will take care of everything for my master.'

And just as Puss had planned, the miller's youngest son got married to the princess in a grand ceremony that had the whole kingdom celebrating for days.

As Puss curled up on her velvet cushion after indulging in a cup of super rich and heavy cream, she grinned at her master.

'Now do you believe that I am your friend and benefactor and will take care of you, young master?'

Her master laughed and stroked her head with love.

'If I can believe a cat can talk, I can believe in anything! Thank you, Puss! And thank you, Father. I have indeed inherited the best! You are the cleverest Puss I have ever met.'

Puss sighed and yawned and settled down for a nice long nap. She had made her master proud indeed. Tricking the rabbits was child's play, tricking the ogre was even easier, and getting the miller's son the princess was the best trick of all!

# Hermes Steals Cows

*Hermes is one of the Greek Gods. He blesses a wide range of human activity, from travel and trade to language and even thievery! In Roman mythology, he is known as Mercury. He is portrayed with a staff, winged sandals, and often also a winged helmet. He is said to have been involved in many adventures, including the killing of the many-eyed giant Panoptes Argos and freeing the God of war, Ares. Hermes is known to have resorted to trickery and deceit to achieve his goals right from his very birth, as we shall see in this story.*

Maia was the daughter of the Titan Atlas and the Oceanid Pleione, and was one of the seven Pleiades nymphs. The beauty of the Pleiades nymphs was well known all over the world, and Maia was the most beautiful of them all. But she was also very shy, and liked the solitude of the mountains, which is why she had made her home there. She lived in a cave all by herself on Mount Cyllene in Arcadia.

But this did not deter the gods. Zeus, God of sky and thunder, fell madly in love with her, and soon, Maia found herself heavy with child. When she gave birth to her son, Hermes, she knew he would be extraordinary. After all, he was the son of Zeus, the king of Gods—the God of all Gods! But what she had not counted on was

Hermes' being such a naughty child!

Dawn was just breaking when Hermes was born. Maia swaddled him and, feeling extremely tired, she fell asleep. After all, the baby was going to be fast asleep most of the time, wasn't he?

But Hermes was no ordinary baby and falling asleep wasn't part of his plans. Being the child of a God, he grew so fast that by mid-morning, he was walking around. Having explored the cave, he grew curious about what lay outside, and just as he ventured out, he came across a tortoise.

A short while later, Maia was woken up by some heavenly music.

'What on earth is that?' She wondered, and when she saw the empty cradle, she panicked. Where was her baby? Had someone stolen him from her? And where on earth was that music coming from? She roused herself wearily, yawning and rubbing her eyes, and stumbled out of her cave.

The sight that greeted her made her stop short in astonishment. Hermes was sitting outside on a little crop of rock, with an angelic smile on his face. He had a strange thing in his hand, the likes of which she had never seen before. Was that an empty tortoise shell? And what were those strings that were stretched across the shell? Were they strings of sheep gut? When Hermes plucked at the strings, the music that emanated was simply divine.

'Hermes!' Maia said in a loud and firm voice. 'What are you doing here? And what is all this?'

Hermes turned at the sound of her voice and bestowed a beautiful smile on her.

'See what I have created all by myself, Mother,' he said, stretching his hand out towards her and displaying the instrument. 'This is a lyre, and it will make the sweetest music you will ever hear.'

'Really? That's all very well,' Maia said with a scowl. 'But you are not even a day old, and here you are, disappearing on me and making merry. Come at once to your bed, or I will tell your father. He will be sure to make you miserable for being so disobedient.'

'Oh Mother!' Hermes sighed dramatically. 'Aren't you even the slightest bit impressed that I've created something so magical? You should be rejoicing at the wonderful son you have! Instead, you are scolding me like I am a naughty child.'

'*Like* a naughty child?' Maia tried to suppress the laughter that bubbled through her. 'You *are* a naughty child. Come at once now, and lie down. I shall bind you to your bed if you don't behave,' she threatened, hiding her smile. Her son was indeed wonderful and impressive—and already such a handful! Heaven help her!

She carried him to his bed and tucked him in after feeding him some nectar. She lay down again, and her eyes closed almost immediately.

Of course, it wasn't long before Hermes became restless again. When her light snoring told him that his mother was fast asleep, he crept out of the cave and took off. He wandered here and there, and then went so far that he reached the pastures of the gods themselves.

'What beautiful cattle!' he murmured when he came upon a large herd that was grazing peacefully. He stopped and stood there, admiring them for a long time.

They belonged to Apollo, but that didn't stop Hermes from desiring them. So what did he do?

'Well, there's only one thing I can do, he said to himself and smirked. 'I'll have to steal them!'

'Come on, come on,' he called out, as he rounded up the cattle and guided them towards his home.

'But these creatures are leaving so many hoofprints that it will only be a matter of time before Apollo traces them and tries to get the herd back,' Hermes thought. 'I must do something to make sure I get a head start.'

Hermes was impressively inventive. He made some dummy hooves from the bark of a fallen oak tree and planted the false hoofprints all over the place. He also made the cattle walk in circles and led them through sand to confuse anyone trying to track them by their hoofprints.

As he was driving the herd onwards, he noticed an old man standing and watching him.

'Hello, sir!' He said, bowing with elaborate deference. 'How are you today?'

'I am very well, my boy,' replied the old man. 'How are you doing? And what, may I ask, are you doing with Apollo's cattle?'

'Oh!' Hermes winked. 'I am just playing a prank on him. Promise me you won't breathe a word of this to anyone?'

'I promise,' the old man said, but didn't meet the boy's eyes. Hermes was immediately on his guard.

'Thank you, kind sir,' he replied. 'And whose acquaintance do I have the pleasure of making?'

'My name is Battus, boy,' the old man replied.

'Ah Battus,' Hermes said, 'do you really promise that you will not tell anyone what you have seen here today? Do I have your word?'

'You do,' the elder man responded and turned away. 'I must be on my way, sorry.'

Hermes became very suspicious at once. His intuition told him that the old man was certainly going to break his promise and report him to Apollo. But how was he to test this feeling of his?

Battus had gone but a little distance when he came across a handsome young man who looked like a soldier.

'Good day, old man,' the youth called out to him. 'Have you by any chance seen a herd of cattle being led away?'

Battus stopped in his tracks, debating whether to spill the beans or not.

'Apollo is offering a handsome reward for information of any sort,' the youth told him. 'It is a very handsome reward indeed. So tell me, have you seen anything?'

Battus was now tempted. He could definitely use the reward, and having Apollo himself owe him one would not be such a bad thing. He made up his mind and nodded.

'Yes,' he replied and pointed in the direction from which he had come. 'I did see a young boy leading a herd of cattle in that direction. I am pretty sure they were Apollo's cattle. He told me it was a prank and asked me not to say anything to anyone.'

'And you gave him your word, did you not?' The young soldier sneered. 'Yet here you are, breaking your promise. You deserve to be punished, not rewarded!'

'How do you know I gave him my word?' Battus stuttered as right before his widening eyes, the youth transformed back to Hermes.

'You broke your word!' Hermes hissed. 'You broke your promise to me. And for that, you will indeed be punished.'

Hermes turned on his heel and strode away, furious at the betrayal. Even as Battus stood there in shock, he turned into a stone statue. Hermes had cursed him.

Soon, Hermes came to the river Alpheus. He knew the price he had to pay for a safe passage across the river.

'I will sacrifice two of my cows,' he said, and prepared them for his sacrifice.

He knew he could not leave any trace of his sacrifice

behind, for that would help anyone trying to track the herd. So he carefully burnt the hooves and the heads and covered all remnants with dirt and weeds, so that it was impossible to even tell that there had been a sacrifice at that site.

Hermes finally reached home. He gathered the cattle into a well-concealed enclosure, deep in the forest. Pleased with his accomplishment, he slipped back into the cave. He went straight to his bed, lay down, and closed his eyes as if in deep slumber.

'Well, well, well,' his mother's voice resonated through the cave. 'The travelling son has returned home at last. And what mischief have you been up to?'

Hermes pretended to wake up from a sound sleep. He opened his eyes, stretching and yawning.

'Travelling, Mother?' He blinked innocently. 'I have been here all along. Have you been dreaming?'

Maia scoffed. 'Hermes, my child, you may think you are very smart, but I am your mother. I know when something is brewing in that naughty little head of yours. I can feel it in my bones that you have done something seriously wicked.'

Her ears pricked up at the distant sound of cattle lowing.

'Hermes!' She said sharply. 'What have you done, my boy?'

'Absolutely nothing, mother!' Hermes protested. 'I have been right here.'

Maia gave him a long, searching look, and sighed.

'You know, you will be in huge trouble with the gods. I know it. I don't know exactly what you've done yet, but I'm pretty sure I'll have some visitors soon, thirsty for your blood. Oh Hermes! Let's hope you survive the wrath of the gods.'

'Oh, trust me, mother, I am sure I will,' Hermes gave her a smug smile, and Maia shook her head in despair.

True to her fears, they had a visitor a short while later.

Apollo strode in, looking thunderous with rage.

'You!' He pointed a stern finger at Hermes. 'You have stolen my cattle. Return them to me at once!'

Hermes took his time to respond. He turned around, blinking his large baby eyes innocently.

'Me? Stealing your cattle? I think you must be mistaken. I was born just this morning. Do you think I am even capable of accomplishing such a feat?'

'You are the one who did it. I was told by an omen, and omens are not to be disbelieved. How dare you deny it?'

'The omen must be wrong,' Hermes pouted. 'I am just a little boy, I cannot have done such a thing. Why, I don't even know what cattle means!'

'Mother,' he turned to Maia and asked in a baby voice, 'what does cattle mean?'

Maia suppressed the laughter that bubbled within and threatened to erupt. Hermes was taking this too far.

'Don't play with me, boy!' Apollo growled. In one swift move, he swooped down and hauled Hermes over his shoulder. 'I'm taking you to your father. Let's see what he has to say about this!'

Hermes struggled to escape, but Apollo's grip was firm. Soon, they stood before Zeus.

'What is all this about?' Zeus frowned. 'Why have you brought my son here?'

'He has stolen my cattle,' Apollo roared. 'And he refuses to confess to it.'

Zeus looked at his son, who had a devilish twinkle in his eyes. He could see straightaway that Apollo was right.

'Hermes, come to my side, my boy,' Zeus ordered.

When his son came to him, Zeus knelt down till he was at eye level with Hermes.

'My dear son,' he said, 'you are extraordinary indeed. I know it, your mother knows it, indeed, the whole world knows it. Let's not allow this prank to get out of hand and cause wars and mayhem. Confess to your prank and lead Apollo to his herd, my child. Do it because your father is telling you to do so.'

Hermes sighed and his shoulders drooped as he turned to Apollo.

'All right, I confess,' he said in a low voice. 'I took your herd of cattle. Come on, I will lead you to it.'

'Thank you very much, Zeus,' Apollo bowed and turned to follow Hermes. 'Lead the way, boy.'

When they reached the hidden enclosure, Apollo counted his cattle. He frowned as he counted them again.

'There are two missing,' he said to Hermes. 'What did you do now?'

'I had to sacrifice them,' Hermes explained, and led Apollo to where the sacrificial meat lay. 'See, I have divided it into twelve equal portions, one for each god.'

'Twelve?' Apollo frowned again. Hermes was too clever by half and Apollo was having a tough time keeping up with him. 'Why twelve? There are only eleven Gods.'

'No, there are twelve,' Hermes said stubbornly.

'Really? Name them!' Apollo challenged.

'Here goes,' said Hermes, with a smile. 'First is Zeus, the king of the Gods. Second, his wife, Hera, goddess of marriage and childbirth. Third is Poseidon, the god of storms and seas. Fourth is Demeter, the goddess of harvests. Fifth is Athena, the goddess of wisdom. Sixth, you yourself, the great Apollo, god of prophecy, medicine and the arts. Seventh is Artemis, the goddess of the hunt. Eighth is Ares, the god of war. Ninth is Aphrodite, the goddess of love and passion. Tenth is Hephaestus, master craftsman and blacksmith. Eleventh is Hestia, goddess of the hearth.'

Hermes paused here, and Apollo smirked.

'See, only eleven gods and goddesses, my boy. You were wrong.'

Hermes shook his head with a broad smile.

'No Apollo, you are wrong. Twelfth is me, Hermes.'

Apollo chuckled at the youth's audacity.

'Is that right? You consider yourself a God?'

'I do,' Hermes drew himself up and looked Apollo in the eye. 'Do you deny it?'

Apollo stared at Hermes with a mixture of admiration and surprise for a long moment. Then he shrugged in acceptance.

'I think it's time to get my cattle home,' he said.

As he gathered the herd together, Hermes sat on a rock nearby and began to play his lyre. Apollo's ears pricked up—after all, he was the god of music as well, and he had never heard such wonderful music before. Hermes began to sing, and Apollo could hardly believe his ears—they were songs praising Apollo and his many admirable attributes! The god shook his head in amusement. Hermes was really too clever by half. No god could resist flattery, could they?

'What is this you have?' Apollo asked, pointing to the lyre.

'Oh, it's just something I invented,' Hermes said dismissively.

'The music it creates is truly magical,' Apollo said. 'Don't you think I ought to be the owner of such a divine instrument, being the god of music and all?'

Hermes looked at him, the mischievous twinkle back in his eyes.

'And what will you give me in return, Apollo?' He asked.

'What do you want?'

'Umm...let me think...what about this herd of cattle?'

Apollo let out a guffaw. 'You are too much, Hermes! Never mind.'

But as he turned away, Hermes played the lyre so enticingly that Apollo could not bear it any longer.

'All right, all right!' He threw up his hands. 'I'll give you this herd of cattle in exchange for the lyre.'

'As you wish, my God,' Hermes bowed and handed over the lyre immediately. He was very pleased indeed with the bargain he had made.

Apollo was leaving when he heard another strange and delightful sound. The notes lingered hauntingly in the air, wrapping everything in a mystical mood. He stopped in his tracks, completely enchanted by the music that echoed through the woods and made every living being pause, entranced.

'Hermes!' He called out, striding back to the

boy-turned-god. 'What do you have now?'

Hermes paused in his playing. In his hands, he held a slender, hollowed reed-pipe with holes in it.

'Oh, this is something I made just now to keep myself amused,' he said, pointing to the pipe. 'It makes a delightful sound, does it not?'

'Indeed it does,' Apollo agreed, 'I must have it.'

'You *must* have it?' Hermes raised an eyebrow. 'Why? I made this for myself.'

'I know,' Apollo said, desperation clear in his voice. 'But I need it, I must have it. I have to have it!'

'And what will you give in exchange?' Hermes smiled, knowing he had Apollo cornered.

'Whatever you want,' Apollo said. 'Ask and it shall be yours.'

'Really? You promise?'

'Yes! Just give that...that thing to me!'

'All right,' Hermes said. 'I want your golden staff.'

'Done.'

'I also want to be the god of shepherds and herdsmen.'

'Done.'

'And I want to be instructed in the use of pebbles to divine the future.'

'What?' Apollo frowned. 'Haven't you asked for enough already?'

'Say yes, if you want this reed pipe.'

'Sweet Zeus!' Apollo ran his hand through his hair. 'You really drive a hard bargain!'

He raised his hands in defeat. 'All right, I agree, you will receive instruction. Now give me the heavenly pipe before I snatch it from you!'

Hermes handed over the pipe to Apollo, all smiles. What an eventful day it had been!

But the day was not over yet. His father had summoned him. Hermes wasted no time in presenting himself, hoping against hope that Zeus was not too angry with him.

'I've been hearing stories,' Zeus began with a frown, 'and I do not like what I am hearing. My son is lying and cheating and stealing? Do you wish to dishonour my name, Hermes? Never again do I want to hear such stories. Promise me that there will be no more of this.'

'I promise, Father,' Hermes bowed, 'but on one condition.'

Zeus looked surprised. 'You are bargaining with *me*?'

Hermes paused and then began. 'Dear Father, you know me and you know my nature. There is but one way to keep me out of trouble—keeping me busy. Keep me so busy that I will have no time for such antics.'

'And how will I keep you busy?' Zeus couldn't suppress his smile. Doubtless, his clever son had already thought of everything.

'Make me your messenger and herald. I will be so busy going from place to place delivering your missives, that I will have no time to get into any mischief.'

Zeus gave his son a broad smile.

'Your wish is granted, son,' he said. 'And I'll give you more. You will be in charge of protecting travellers, since you will come to know all the world's paths intimately, travelling them yourself. You will be the god of negotiating treaties, seeing that you have a knack for striking very good bargains, fair to all sides. And last but not least, because of your proficiency at trading, you shall also oversee the promotion of trade as well.'

Hermes' eyes widened in surprise. His father's words both astonished and pleased him immensely.

'Thank you, Father!' He laughed. 'Thank you!'

'And as icing on the cake, here are some gifts for you,' Zeus smiled affectionately at Hermes and dropped a package into his arms.

'What...what is all this?' Hermes spluttered, truly taken aback. He had come assuming that he would be reprimanded, and that he would have to fight for what he wanted. He certainly hadn't expected to be showered with gifts.

'Wow!' He held up golden sandals which had little wings on their sides.

'For your speedy travels,' Zeus said.

'This is so awesome!' Hermes held up a little round headpiece.

'To protect you from the rain.'

'And a herald's staff!' Hermes breathed deeply, trying to contain his excitement, as he stroked a beautiful staff which had two entwined serpents carved on it.

'Go on, my son,' Zeus said. 'God speed!'

# Reynard Tricks the King

*Stories about Reynard the Fox abound in European folklore. They are popular across English, Dutch, French and German cultures. Reynard is cunning and will not stop at anything to get what he wants. He is a master of trickery and deceit and loves to sow seeds of discord wherever he goes. Often his stories are seen as representative of society, which, in his time, was made up of the royalty, the knighthood, the religious institutions and the common masses. Reynard knows exactly how to navigate these layers and come out on top. The story here is an excerpt from one of the many longer tales.*

The great feast at the palace of King Noble promised to be the biggest extravaganza anyone had ever witnessed. The air was replete with the aroma of the most delicious food: tables were groaning under the weight of tureens of rich meats, velvety sauces, succulent fruit, and scrumptious desserts; and wines flowed freely. Servants scurried back and forth, bringing more juicy treats every minute. Musicians strummed and drummed, adding to the cacophony. The attendees were also ecstatic.

'I hope you are all enjoying this feast,' King Noble roared aloud over the din in the great hall. 'I am delighted that you could join me. You can share anything you want with me today, for the wine loosens the tongue, and I will not hold it against you,' he winked and the whole hall reverberated with guffaws and laughter.

Isengrim the Wolf had been waiting all along for just such an opportunity. He absolutely hated Reynard the Fox, and had a long list of grievances against him. So, he waited for the feast to resume, before making his way to the king. Accompanying him were those whom he had picked and chosen, for he knew they too detested Reynard, and wanted him gone from the court.

'Your Majesty,' he bowed, as he addressed the lion.

'Ah Isengrim! How are you doing this fine day? I hope you are enjoying the feast?'

'I am, Your Majesty,' the wolf replied. 'What a feast you have thrown! This will surely be remembered for generations to come!'

King Noble knew that Isengrim had not approached him just to praise the event.

'Come now, Isengrim. I see that you have come with an entourage. I think you wish to share something with me that's unrelated to the feast. Am I right?'

Isengrim had the grace to look ashamed.

'Indeed, Your Majesty,' he stuttered. 'You are too clever; you have read my mind.'

'Out with it, Isengrim. I am ready to hear whatever you have to say.'

'It is Reynard the Fox, Your Majesty. He is cruel and cunning and given to trick all of us all the time. I think he is the reason my children have gone blind. And it's not just me that he has injured. All my companions have similar horror stories about Reynard.'

Isengrim nudged the hare standing next to him.

Panther's nose quivered as he started, but he picked up the wolf's cue.

'Yes indeed, Your Majesty. He had told me he would teach me prayers, but as soon as I closed my eyes, he grabbed me by my neck, and if his grip hadn't been loose, I would have been dead by now!' Panther's eyes grew wide in distress, and he could not stop trembling.

'And the evil fox promised me that he was no longer eating meat, and yet he tried to make off with one of my chicks!' Chanticleer the rooster stepped forward, his red crest looking angrier than ever, and his voice booming over the noise of the feast.

'He is a real troublemaker, Your Majesty,' Isengrim took over once again. 'He has caused all of us a lot of problems. We are very worried that he will soon wreak havoc in the kingdom, and trouble will land up at your doorstep too.'

'Hmmm,' said King Noble, pondering over the complaints. 'I have never had a problem with Reynard the Fox. I have always found him to be polite and intelligent. However, I cannot dismiss what you are saying, especially given the many complaints. I will summon him to court to cross-examine him and give him a chance to defend himself. If your accusations prove true, then he will face the severest punishment imaginable. You can trust me on that.'

'You are brave, just and fair, Your Majesty!' Isengrim bowed, hiding his grin. His companions bowed with him. His work was done, and Reynard the Fox was in big trouble now.

Tibert the Cat and Gimbard the Brock were close by. They had overheard all that had transpired. They hurried up to King Noble once Isengrim and his companions had left.

'Your Majesty,' Tibert said, bowing low. 'We could not help hearing what Isengrim has been filling your ears with. I cannot help but protest. He is guilty of far worse crimes than Reynard, and has a long-standing grudge against the fox, who is too smart for him. All he wants to do is get his revenge.'

'That is true, Your Majesty,' Gimbard interjected. 'I have heard Isengrim swearing his vengeance on Reynard many-a-time. He persuades his friends to take his side and ignore all the evil he himself unleashes. We trust you will take what Isengrim says with a large pinch of salt.'

King Noble raised his eyebrows at Tibert and Gimbard. He knew trouble was brewing in the court, but he didn't know that matters were getting so out of hand.

'I shall summon Reynard to court and give him a chance to explain himself,' he said thoughtfully. 'If I am convinced, I will set him free. Otherwise, I will punish him so severely that he will serve as an example for the rest of my subjects to not take advantage of my leniency.'

Tibert and Gimbard looked at each other. This reprieve would have to do. Reynard had better get his explanations ready. He would have to do a mighty good job of convincing King Noble that he was innocent of all that he had been accused of.

The next day, Bruin the Bear set off towards Reynard's castle. He had been instructed by the king to get Reynard to court, and pay no attention to any excuses that Reynard might offer. It was a long and tedious journey, and by the time Bruin arrived at the castle, he was hungry and irritable. He longed for a delicious meal and a restful nap. But he knew that the king would brook no delays, so he hastened to announce himself to the guards.

'Bruin, my good man!'

Reynard was lying sprawled on a couch, his eyes nearly closing. He didn't even bother to get up to greet Bruin, and this annoyed the bear even more. Such insolence! He would report all this to the king and make sure Reynard got what he deserved!

'Reynard,' Bruin said in a patient, long-suffering voice. 'You must have already heard that King Noble requires your presence immediately at his court. I have been sent to inform you and accompany you back. If you do not do as the king says and prepare to leave at once, the consequences would be dire, believe me.'

'Dear me!' Reynard said, trying to raise himself unsuccessfully from the couch. 'You say King Noble requires my presence immediately? Oh, I wish you had come just an hour earlier.'

'And why is that?' Bruin demanded impatiently.

'It's just that I have feasted on the most exquisite honey ever!' Reynard sighed. 'It was so good that I overindulged myself, and see now, how I lie helpless and unable to move, having filled my belly so full that I am not even able to rise to greet you. I am truly sorry, but you must give me a little time so that I can feel better.'

Bruin grumbled under his breath.

'Bruin, I am sorry to waste your time. But I can offer

you something to make up for it. Would you want to feast on the honey as well? I can guide you to where it is, and you can help yourself to your heart's content. By that time, I should have recovered too, and we can set off to the king's court.'

Bruin smiled. Now this was something he could definitely do.

'I would be most happy to do that, Reynard,' he chortled. 'I think it would be perfect.'

Now Reynard had absolutely no plans to accompany Bruin to court. He knew through his spies that King Noble was not very happy with him. So he gave directions to the bear to a copse in the woods where he knew hunters had set a trap.

'I'm sure you'll enjoy the feast of honey!' he called after the bear, who trotted off eagerly to devour his favourite food to his heart's content.

Unfortunately, just as Reynard had planned, Bruin landed in the trap set by the hunters. He twisted this way and that, trying his best to escape from the people who circled him and beat him mercilessly. Glimpsing a gap in the ring, Bruin lunged towards it and ran away as fast as he could, putting as great a distance between himself and the hunters as possible. He ran long and hard till he arrived back at the King's court.

'And have you brought Reynard with you?' King Noble looked at Bruin crossly. The poor bear was exhausted and could hardly stand. But he dared not collapse in front of the king.

'I'm sorry, Your Majesty, but I was tricked and...'

'Enough!' roared the king. 'I have had enough of miserable weaklings like you who cannot even do the simplest of tasks assigned to them. Begone from my sight before I lose control, otherwise you will be punished so badly that you will never see the light of day!'

Bruin scurried away, glad to have not lost his skin to the king's wrath. Damn that fox, he thought.

'Hmmm, Reynard has proven again that he can outwit anyone,' the king mused. 'I need to find the right person to haul him to court; someone who will not fall for his tricks.'

The next day, Tibert the cat was sent as the king's envoy to Reynard. The instructions were strict: bring Reynard to the court immediately, no excuses.

Tibert the cat approached Reynard's castle cautiously. He wasn't an enemy of the fox, and had, in fact, defended him in front of the king on several occasions. But this time was different. He knew he could not save Reynard from the king's fury. He only hoped the fox would be smart enough to understand his options, and to choose the correct course of action—which was to surrender to the king.

'Ah! My friend Tibert! I am so glad to see you at my castle. What brings you here?' Reynard enquired graciously with a welcoming embrace.

'I regret that I have rather grim news for you, Reynard,' Tibert announced, stepping back. He didn't want to encourage any friendliness between the two of them for fear of jeopardizing his mission. 'You have made King Noble very, very angry indeed. You didn't make matters any better by tricking Bruin when he was sent to bring you in. Now the king demands that you surrender immediately, and present yourself at court.

Disobey his command, and you will face the penalty of death. I have been sent to accompany you. Please prepare to leave immediately.'

Reynard's face clouded for a moment before he slapped Tibert on the back.

'Consider your message conveyed and received, my friend!' He said with a broad smile. 'But you have made a long and tiring journey, so, first and foremost, I must play the gracious host.'

Tibert began to protest, but Reynard shook his head.

'I know what you said about leaving immediately, but come on, between you and me, a few minutes this way or that will hardly make a difference. Besides, given what looms on the horizon, there is no way of knowing when this opportunity will come my way again—for me to play host to you and ply you with a feast equal to our friendship. Come, my friend, Tibert, don't be so adamant. It is just so that you can rest a little and refresh yourself before we leave to face another ordeal at court.'

Tibert could hardly resist Reynard's persuasive charm. A small meal, a tiny drink, and a little nap would be very nice indeed.

'Well, if you insist,' Tibert succumbed to the temptation. 'Lead the way. But I warn you again, this delay ought to only be for a few minutes, else King Noble will skin me alive.'

Reynard hid a smile.

'Of course, of course,' he agreed. 'I have arranged a modest feast of the juiciest rats and mice my fellows could catch. I am sure you will enjoy it. It will be just the thing you need before we make the long journey back.'

Tibert drooled at the mention of the feast. He

hurried behind Reynard, who led him into an open courtyard and pointed to its centre. Without a second thought, he ran in the direction of Reynard's finger in excited anticipation.

Imagine his utter shock when he was suddenly flung into the air before landing in a net that closed snugly around him!

'Reynard!' He bellowed. 'What have you done?'

Reynard chuckled and shook his head, before disappearing from sight. Tibert yowled in anger. The fox had set a trap and betrayed him! He had thought of him as a friend, but now he could never, ever trust him again.

The next day saw an exhausted and bedraggled Tibert drag himself to the court. He had managed to escape, but now feared for his very life. One look at him, and King Noble exploded in fury.

'Grimbard!' He hollered. The brock appeared at once in front of him. 'Go at once and drag that cunning fox, Reynard, to court. Don't listen to his excuses and don't fall for his tricks. Bring him here and let him feel the full force of my wrath!'

This time, Reynard too knew that there was no way out. He accompanied Grimbard to court without creating a fuss, but his mind was working overtime on finding a way out of this mess. At the court too, a retinue of courtiers, led, of course, by Isengrim the Wolf, stepped forward to accuse him of all sorts of crimes. As the list of his misdemeanours grew, Reynard became more and more anxious. King Noble looked extremely grim and serious, and was in no mood to even listen, much less forgive. At the end of the lengthy session, the king looked at Reynard with narrowed eyes.

'You, Reynard the Fox, have been causing too much harm and injury to your fellow men. You have caused them grievous damage, some of which they can never recover from. You have proven to be a menace to society. I hereby pronounce your sentence: you are to be hanged tomorrow!'

A loud cheer greeted the king's verdict and applause followed as the king rose and left the court.

'Come, you filthy fox!' The guards grabbed at Reynard and dragged him to the dungeons, even as his enemies spat and snarled and hurled the choicest abuses at him. There was not a single friend left in the assembly, and Reynard's heart sank. Was he really going to be hanged tomorrow? Was that how all this would end?

The next morning, a jeering crowd gathered around the gallows, waiting for the disgraced Reynard to be brought out. But when the wily fox emerged accompanied by guards, he didn't look ashamed, upset, or even guilty. No, in fact, he looked well-rested and even had a smile upon his face! The puzzled folk began to whisper amongst themselves. What was the meaning of all this?

King Noble arrived soon after, and once the hubbub died down, he addressed Reynard.

'Reynard, you have been accused of the most dastardly crimes. You will shortly be hanged to death. Do you have anything to say for yourself?'

'I do, Your Majesty,' Reynard bowed low. 'I have indeed been accused of such imaginative crimes that even I could not have dreamed them up. And I confess that I am guilty of each and every crime. I repeat—I. AM. GUILTY!'

A roar emanated from the crowd, and the guards had to threaten violence to maintain order.

'But do I deserve to be hanged for them? Absolutely not, Your Majesty. For I have done all these crimes, and made all these enemies, and risked my very life because of just one reason, and one reason alone.'

Reynard paused dramatically here, milking the suspense for all its worth.

'And that reason is...to save YOU, Your Majesty!'

'What?' King Noble's jaw dropped in disbelief. 'Explain yourself!' He demanded.

Reynard spoke quickly.

'You are surrounded by enemies, Your Majesty. You already know of this, but you do not know just how close they have come to ending your reign. Trust me, I have kept a close eye on them at very great personal risk. Even now, my accusers have almost succeeded in getting me out of their way in their nefarious plans to assassinate you by convincing you that I should be hanged to death.

'Your Majesty, your enemies have amassed a vast hoard of gold and jewels. They are planning to use this in a grave conspiracy to usurp the throne. I have used every trick in my bag to seize control of this treasure. I am tired of all this skulduggery and scheming, and I am ready to turn over the treasure to you right away. I have always worked for you, Your Majesty. If you do not believe me and still wish to hang me, please do so right away. I will leave you to your own devices, since you choose not to accept my helping hand. Hang me, if that is what you desire, and let your enemies win. Is that what you really want? Set me free, and *you* will win. The treasure will be yours and your enemies will vanish faster than you can imagine.'

Reynard took a deep breath, and bowed low again.

'That is all I have to say, Your Majesty. Now your wish is my command.'

He stood as still as a statue, even though chaos churned around him. The courtiers were screaming themselves hoarse and the crowd was chanting all sorts of slogans. King Noble's face grew redder and redder as he tried to work a way out of this fix.

Reynard looked calm, but inside, he was in turmoil. He prayed hard for his ploy to work. There certainly wasn't any treasure, nor was there any conspiracy to assassinate the king, but this was the only idea he could come up with to get out of this situation alive. Knowing how greedy the king was, Reynard hoped that the treasure would be enough temptation for the king to let him go free. Still, if things went wrong, this would be Reynard's last day on earth.

King Noble raised his hand, and a silence fell over the gathering.

'I have known Reynard for a long time, and I have always been impressed by his wily ways. His cunning goes a long way in ensuring survival in dangerous times. I have seen him do this before, and I am witnessing it today. Should I believe him and set him free? Or is he lying, and ought he to be hanged?'

The king paused, and the entire kingdom held its breath.

'Reynard, consider it your lucky day, for I believe you. I am setting you free, but on one strict condition: you turn in the treasure you have amassed in my name to its rightful owner—me. Do so immediately, or you will once again be arrested, and this time you will be hanged for certain.'

The king's announcement was greeted with great clamour. Only Reynard stood in the centre of it all, a smirk on his face.

Once again, his sharp wits had helped him escape the jaws of death by the skin of his teeth.

But this is not the end of the story. Reynard succeeds in outwitting the king again and again. This was just the beginning.

# Ivan the Fool

*Ivan the Fool is often used as a general term for simpletons in Russian culture. However, it is also the title of a short story by the great Russian author Leo Tolstoy. The story here is an excerpt from Tolstoy's tale, which is a complex one representing several angles and reflecting society in general. In this story, Ivan the Fool 'tricks' the Devil himself, not through any elaborate ruses, but through the goodness and simplicity of his heart.*

A well-off peasant in a village had three sons and a daughter.

The eldest son Simeon was a soldier in the Czar's army. The second son Tarras-Briukhan was a merchant who was doing very well. The third son Ivan was often dismissed as a fool, since he had remained in the village and showed no interest in worldly matters. He and his sister Milania, who was born mute, worked for their father on the family farm. Ivan had no complaints about his life, and he went about his work with sincerity.

Simeon's wife was prone to spending extravagantly, and he soon ran out of money. So he returned to his father's house and insisted on his share of the family money. His father was reluctant to distribute his wealth while he was still alive. Since Ivan worked with his father, and Simeon did not contribute anything to the household, his father asked Ivan if he had any objections to fulfilling Simeon's request. Ivan had no objections, so Simeon was given his share.

Tarras was not satisfied with the wealth he was earning. When he heard that Simeon had got his share of the family money, Tarras too demanded his share. Again, Ivan had no objections, and his father gave Tarras his share.

Now, The Devil (a term used by folks to refer to harmful, malignant, and unclean spirits) was watching all this with interest. Since his interest in worldly matters always revolved around conflict, damage, distress and negative emotions, he was greatly disappointed when the brothers did not fight each other over the family money.

'I need to provoke a fight among the brothers,' The Devil mused. Then he called out to three imps. The imps were small and bony and awful to look at. The first imp had grey mottled skin, ears that flapped like fans, and long claws. The second imp had a long snout with sharp teeth bared in an evil grin, and a tail with a nasty sharp end. The third imp had pointy horns, large stinky blisters all over, and ragged prickly wings. A nasty looking trio for sure!

'Come here, you little devils,' he chortled as they lined up before him in a murky swamp. 'Let's go and stir up some trouble in his household. 'You,' he pointed to the first imp, 'will take on Simeon'. 'You,' he said, pointing to the second imp, 'will be in charge of Tarras. 'And you,' he pointed to the third imp, 'you will take on Ivan. I need you to go out there and make things as ugly as you can. What's the fun in peace and harmony?

Go on, do me proud, you little devils!' He sent them on their way, and rubbed his hands in gleeful anticipation.

'I think I'm going to do a great job,' said Imp One.

'I think I'm going to do a superb job,' said Imp Two.

'I'm not so sure. Unfortunately I've got Ivan the Fool,' sighed Imp Three. 'Can you two help me?'

'I don't think we can,' said Imp One. 'We'll be too busy handling our own cases, but in case one of us finishes early, we can come by and help you.'

'That's fine by me,' agreed Imp Two. 'Let's meet near this swamp again and compare notes.'

A few days later, the imps met again to exchange notes on their progress.

Imp One looked triumphant. 'Messing with Simeon was a breeze! I first made him so full of himself that he went up to the Czar and offered to lead a very important battle. Then, I made the enemy soldiers so strong with a magic drink that Simeon and his army were utterly defeated. I made sure he got clobbered. So now Simeon is in complete and utter disgrace and is hiding at home!'

Imp Two couldn't wait to share his news either. 'Tarras was a cakewalk, I tell you! All I did was make him crazy with greed. Soon enough, he emptied his coffers. Now collectors are beating on his door, and he is all shrivelled up with shame and hiding at home!'

Imp One and Imp Two high-fived each other.

Imp Three let out a long-suffering sigh.

'As I predicted, I failed completely. I first made Ivan sick, but that didn't stop him from going to work. Then, I made the earth as hard as I could. I also broke one of the blades of his plough, and held on to the blade as firmly as I could, but even that didn't stop Ivan the

Fool from ploughing almost the entire field. Instead, I got my hands all cut up for my trouble. I am definitely going to need your help,' Imp Three concluded gloomily.

The next day, Ivan woke up early because he had to finish ploughing the last bit of the field. Even though he felt dreadfully sick, he was determined to complete his work. But strangely, his plough would not budge even though he pushed with all his might.

'This is so strange,' Ivan thought. 'There are no roots here to block its path. Then what could be causing the obstruction?' He put his hand into the earth, and pulled out something strange. Struggling within his palm, was an imp! He curled his hand into a fist, ready to punch it dead, when it cried out loud.

'Please let me go. I will give you anything you ask for.'

Ivan stopped in surprise. 'What?'

'Anything you wish, I can grant you. Please don't kill me.'

'Well,' Ivan scratched his beard, 'perhaps you can cure me of this dreadful sick feeling I have in my stomach. Nothing has helped it.'

The imp produced some roots. 'Here, take this, it will cure any illness at once.'

Ivan broke off a bit of the root, and just as the imp had promised, his pain immediately disappeared.

'Very well then,' Ivan said, 'you have kept your word, so I will set you free. May God bless you!'

Just as Ivan mentioned God's name, the imp disappeared in a flash. He had vanished because the name of God was fatal to imps, who were servants of the Devil.

When Ivan returned home, he was surprised to see Simeon and his wife at the table. Having narrowly evaded capture, they were seeking refuge in his father's house. Ivan greeted them with a smile and went about his business.

Since Simeon had been taken care of, Imp One went in search of Imp Three to assist him in tackling Ivan. But Imp Three seemed to have vanished altogether.

'Very well,' said Imp One to himself. 'I will handle Ivan all by myself.'

Ivan was to cut the grass in the meadow, and had been sharpening his scythe in preparation. Imp One promptly flooded the entire meadow overnight, and the next morning, when Ivan arrived, the grass proved impossible to cut.

'This is ridiculous,' Ivan said. 'I will sharpen my scythe again and return. I vow to have the grass mown one way or another.'

When Ivan returned, Imp One clung to his scythe so hard that it could barely move. Yet Ivan persisted. He mowed the rye, then the oats, working through the night to make up for lost time. Frustrated, Imp One cursed and resolved to sow rot in the freshly-cut grain instead. But all this constant effort to keep up with Ivan had tired him out, and he dozed off.

A sharp pain in his back woke him up, and he jumped awake with a loud yelp.

'You again?' Ivan glared at him, his pitchfork poised to strike the same spot where it had already jabbed Imp One once.

'No! No!' Imp One cried, alarmed. 'I am with Simeon. It was my brother who was with you.'

'I don't care, you little devil,' Ivan growled, raising his pitchfork once again.

'Please don't kill me. I'll give you anything you want. Just let me go,' Imp One pleaded.

'And what can you do for me?' Ivan asked.

'I can make soldiers out of straw.'

'And how will that be of any help to me? Can they sing?'

'Of course. Whatever you want. Just scatter some straw and see.'

Ivan took some straws and scattered them on the ground. To his amazement, they turned into soldiers and started marching to a band.

'Now will you please let me go?' Imp One asked hopefully.

'Not before you turn the soldiers back to straw,

which is what I really need,' Ivan said. Imp One did just that.

'Very well then,' Ivan said, 'you have kept your word, so I will set you free. May God bless you!'

Just as Ivan mentioned God's name, Imp One disappeared in a flash. He too had been wiped out.

When he returned home, Ivan was surprised to see Tarras and his wife at the table. They too were seeking refuge in his father's house. Ivan greeted them with a smile, and went about his business.

Since Tarras had been taken care of, Imp Two went in search of Imp Three to assist him in tackling Ivan. But both Imp One and Imp Three seemed to have vanished altogether.

'Very well,' said Imp Two to himself. 'I will handle Ivan all by myself.'

Ivan was preparing to chop some wood to build new cabins. There were too many people at home now and it was getting rather crowded. Ivan supposed he could easily chop at least fifty trees in one day. But Imp Two created such trouble that he was barely able to chop ten trees.

'This is ridiculous,' Ivan said as he sank to the ground in exhaustion. 'My back is paining so badly, I don't know how I will finish.'

This made Imp Two chortle with glee. 'Give up, Ivan. Just give up and go home,' he whispered.

But Ivan was nothing if not persistent, and all of a sudden, he stood up and attacked the tree with a great blow. The tree crashed to the ground, and Ivan made such quick work of chopping up all the branches that Imp Two had no time to escape before he was spotted.

'You again?' Ivan glared at him, his axe ready to fall on the little devil.

'No! No!' Imp Two cried, alarmed. 'I am with Tarras. It was my brother who was with you.'

'I don't care, you little devil,' Ivan growled, raising his axe once again.

'Please don't kill me. I'll give you anything you want. Just let me go,' Imp Two pleaded.

'And what can you do for me?' Ivan asked.

'I can make all the money you want. Here, just take the leaves of this oak tree and rub them.'

As Ivan rubbed the oak leaves, he was astonished to see pieces of gold dropping to the ground.

'Now will you please let me go?' Imp Two asked hopefully.

'Very well then,' Ivan said, 'you have kept your word, so I will set you free. May God bless you!'

Just as Ivan mentioned God's name, Imp Two also disappeared in a flash. Like the two others before him, he too had been wiped out.

Soon, all the work on the farm was done and the brothers moved into their own cabins. Ivan then decided to throw a great feast and invite all the villagers to celebrate. Simeon and Tarras turned up their noses at the invitation—they were too posh to dine and dance with these stupid foolish villagers!

The feast was grand and noisy, and there was much to eat and drink. Ivan drank so much that he became quite intoxicated and began to say all sorts of things.

'You must sing my praises,' he said to the lads and lasses. 'I can show you sights that you have never seen before!'

And true to his promise, Ivan did. He scattered straw on the ground and they turned into a marvellous marching band of soldiers. He rubbed oak leaves and threw the gold pieces into the crowd. He caused such chaos that there was almost a stampede, with people climbing over each other, trying to collect the gold.

Of course, the incredible stories soon reached the ears of Ivan's brothers.

'Tell me where you got the soldiers, Ivan!' Simeon demanded.

'Why?' Ivan asked innocently.

'With soldiers, we can conquer entire kingdoms!' Simeon exclaimed.

'I can make as many soldiers as you wish, dear brother. You only have to ask,' Ivan said with a smile. Simeon was delighted with the army Ivan conjured, and off he went to do battle and conquer new kingdoms.

'Tell me where you got the gold, Ivan!' Tarras demanded.

'Why?' Ivan asked innocently.

'With gold, I can gather all the wealth in the world!' Tarras exclaimed.

'I can make as much gold as you wish, dear brother. You only have to ask,' Ivan said with a smile. Tarras filled his wagons with gold and rode away to the city to make even more wealth for himself.

After a while, the two elder brothers met each other. They exchanged stories and decided to ask Ivan to make even more soldiers and gold.

This time however, Ivan declined to assist them.

'Your soldiers kill people so cruelly. I will not create

more soldiers so that you can kill even more people,' he told Simeon.

'A friend had a cow at home, and her children always had plenty of milk to drink. But when a clerk offered her gold, she was tempted and sold the cow, and now her children have no milk to drink. I will not make more gold for you so that you can tempt more people,' he told Tarras.

Simeon and Tarras looked at each other helplessly.

'What do we do now?' Tarras asked, looking anxious.

'Don't worry,' Simeon said, 'I have an idea. Why don't we share our possessions? I will give you half my kingdom and soldiers. They can look after your gold. You can pay me for it with half your gold. That is a fair deal for both of us, isn't it?'

Tarras nodded. In this way, both brothers became rulers of their own kingdoms, and they prospered.

Ivan, however, still continued to stay on the farm and help out. One might say that he was a fool to do so. He could have easily created countless soldiers to conquer kingdoms and heaps of gold to become the richest man in the world, but he was content to be on the farm.

One day, their old dog grew sick, and Ivan remembered the magical roots that Imp Three had given him. When he fed a bit of the root to their pet, the dog was immediately cured.

'How did this happen?' asked everyone curiously, and Ivan told them all about the magic roots.

Soon after, news of the Czar's daughter falling seriously ill reached the village. Everyone naturally turned to Ivan.

'You have the magic roots, you can cure her, you must go!' They all urged him.

Ivan agreed. When he had packed everything and was all set to head to the capital, an old beggar woman knocked on the door.

'I am very, very ill, please help me,' she gasped, as she almost collapsed on the threshold.

Without any hesitation, Ivan produced the magic root and gave it to the beggar woman. As expected, she miraculously recovered.

'God bless you!' She cried with tears in her eyes.

'But you now have no magic root left for the Czar's daughter, Ivan!' cried his father in dismay. 'What are you going to do?'

'Never mind, I shall do my best, father. Please bless me,' Ivan bowed, taking leave of his father.

Ivan had no idea what he would do when he met the Czar or his daughter, or indeed, how he would help her recover. But to his utter astonishment, just as he appeared on the balcony of the Czar's palace, the word spread that the Czar's daughter had been cured!

There was great rejoicing, and the Czar insisted that Ivan was the person who had cured his daughter. The Czar also insisted that Ivan marry his daughter. The Czar also promised that Ivan would inherit the throne once he passed away. Now Ivan the Fool had become Czar! Ivan was no fool. He had defeated the pranks of the imps, tricked them into giving him gifts, and had used the gifts wisely to help create the best life for himself and his family.

And thus, the three brothers became three rulers of their very own kingdoms.

But what of The Devil? After all his efforts to provoke fights and disrupt the peace were brought to naught, he must have been so frustrated and unhappy, right? Did he give up and retire? Or did he come up with some new scheme and succeed in tricking the brothers into an all-out war? For that, you must read the entire story by the world-renowned author Leo Tolstoy, for this is just the beginning of the enchanting tale he has written. Read it, and find out for yourself if Ivan the Fool outwitted The Devil himself!

# Slowing the Sun

*Maui is a Polynesian god. He appears in folktales from islands across the Pacific, including Hawaii. He is often depicted as a naughty rascal with shape-shifting abilities. His representations vary greatly from nation to nation. One of the remarkable things about folktales is how they use human imagination to explain natural phenomena. One such story is about how the sun was slowed down so that humans could have longer summer days. Isn't that just lovely?*

Who hasn't heard of Hawaii? The perfect place to laze around in the sun, go swimming in the blue waters, and watch the most beautiful sunrises and sunsets. Do you know who made 'sunny' Hawaii possible? It was Maui, the Hawaiian demigod. He is known to be a powerful god and quite a trickster—always using his cleverness and ability to shape-shift to accomplish the impossible. He had once been brave enough to lasso the very sun and slow its journey across the skies, so that the people of Hawaii could have longer days and more hours of sunlight. How did he accomplish this? Let's read on to find out.

Maui had four elder brothers who were tall, strong and tough. They often didn't include Maui in their pursuits, and Maui was forever resorting to pranks to join them.

One evening, along with their sister, Hina, they were preparing their evening meal. As they gathered around the fire, heating the stones to cook their meal, it grew dark all of a sudden.

'Why does this happen every day?' Maui grumbled. 'We never have enough light to prepare our meal and always have to eat it in the dark.'

'Tell me about it,' Hina agreed. 'Every day I end up having to wear damp clothes because the sun is never shining long enough to dry out my clothes. At this rate, I won't be surprised if I catch a fever or a cold.'

All the family members nodded. The sun travelled across the sky so quickly that they had barely four hours of sunlight to finish their chores. They were tired of having to move around and work in the dim glow of firelight.

'This will simply not do!' Maui declared, standing up in anger. 'We need the sun's light and heat to live our lives. Why is he in such a hurry to cross the sky? He needs to slow down.'

'Who will catch him and tell him?' asked one of the brothers with a laugh. 'Surely there is no way to get close to the sun without burning ourselves. And even if we could do so, do you think he would even listen to us?'

'We will need to make him listen to us,' Maui said after some deep thought. '*I* will make him listen to us.'

'Are you crazy?' Hina asked anxiously. 'If the sun gets angry with us, he could burn us to ashes in an instant. He will destroy us with his flames of fury. It is impossible.'

'Do you doubt my abilities?' Maui drew himself up, standing tall and broad against the darkness. His muscles rippled with strength; his hard abdomen and strong thighs exuded a strength that could only be divine.

'Do I need to remind you of all my achievements? I took fire from Mahuika when everyone said it was impossible. I descended into the underworld when everyone said it was impossible. I caught the greatest fish in the world when everyone said it was impossible. Do you still think it is impossible for me to catch the sun and order him to slow down?'

A sombre silence fell over the group. What Maui said was true. He had achieved so many seemingly impossible feats earlier. Who was to say that he could not slow the sun down?

A radiant glow emanated from the tall and handsome demigod as he stood like a colossus. He drew from his belt the sacred jawbone of his ancestor and held it high above his head. His voice resonated with an inspired determination.

'I swear upon all that is sacred, I will not rest till I have conquered the sun, till I have slowed the sun, and till the day lasts longer and sunlight stretches into many hours! I swear upon this sacred jawbone of my ancestor that I will not rest until I have accomplished this task. Are you with me?'

The crowd that had gathered around him roared their agreement and their voices resounded like the battle-cry of a victorious army. They were all ready, and they would all help Maui achieve his goal, no matter how difficult it proved to be.

'What do you want us to do, Maui?' his brothers asked him. 'Tell us. We are ready to do your bidding.'

Maui thought for a bit. Then he stood up, ready to make an announcement to the gathering.

'First of all, I would like to thank you all for placing your trust in me. I shall endeavour to the best of my abilities not to betray that trust. I have conceived of a plan. We all know that the sun is proud and burns with arrogance. He will not listen to us, even if we go down on our knees and plead with him. What we need to do is to trap him so that he has no choice but to listen to us. If we need to trap him, we need to build a snare. And for that, I need to make a snare that is strong enough to hold him, yet easy enough for us to construct. The best material for this is flax ropes. So our first step will be to go and collect as much flax as we can. Then we make our ropes, build our trap, and then, finally, we trap the sun and make him listen to us.'

The people who had gathered were hanging on to Maui's every word. They were impressed with his brilliant idea and his careful planning. They had no doubt that he would accomplish what he was setting out to do.

'So now, my dear people,' Maui continued after a pause. 'Go forth and gather as much flax as you can lay your hands on. Make sure the flax is strong and supple, not weak or brittle. You should start right now.'

The folks murmured their approval and began to move away. They were all hard workers, and Maui's brothers were the most swift and skilled. Very soon, mounds of flax began to dot the surface of the islands and then these mounds began to grow in size. Maui himself supervised the sorting of the flax so that the strands that were similar in length and size were grouped together.

As the piles of flax grew to almost twice a man's height, Maui showed another smaller group how to braid the flax into thick strong ropes. Hina had taught him to braid. Now she lent him strands of her own sacred hair which possessed supernatural strength. The flax was being braided almost as fast as it could be gathered. By the time the sun dipped towards the horizon, great lengths of flax rope were coiled into gigantic heaps. Maui surveyed the scene with satisfaction. Everything was going according to plan, and he was pleased.

Once all the flax were braided, Maui gathered the strong young men and women among them.

'Come on,' he said, heaving a great big coil of flax rope onto his shoulders. 'It is time now to go where the sun sleeps. He sleeps in a cave hidden deep in the forest. We need to catch him right there. Follow me closely and do not fall behind, for we don't have much time. Listen to my instructions carefully, for I will be whispering them. Be strong, be patient, and be very, very careful.'

The group moved silently and swiftly through the darkness, despite the heavy flax ropes they were carrying. Maui led the way, heading unerringly towards the cave where the sun rested. When they almost reached their destination, he signalled to them to stop.

'The cave is just a hundred feet away,' he whispered. 'We need to build our snare at the mouth of the cave, so that the sun cannot leave his resting place. We need to camouflage it so that the trap is not visible to the sun as he prepares to rise into the morning. We also need to protect ourselves from the heat of the sun.'

The men and women nodded. If the sun saw the trap, he would immediately know that there was trouble afoot, and would begin to throw out great flaming bolts which would incinerate them on the spot. They would have to be very smart about setting up the trap.

Maui drew the plan of the snare in the mud with a stick, and the group got started. They worked without pause, twisting and coiling and tying up the flax ropes into an intricate net that would well and truly trap the sun. Then they approached the mouth of the cave cautiously and spread the net out, covering it with mud and leaves so that it could not be seen. The ends of the ropes were spread and tucked into the bushes, where the group members would be holding them, ready to pull and capture the sun on Maui's command. The last thing they did was cover themselves with thick layers of clay, for if they did not protect themselves in this way, they would be burnt to ashes in an instant by the sun's immense heat. Once everything was done and everyone was in their assigned place, all they could do was wait. They waited in silence for Maui's signal, their hearts pulsing with a mix of courage and fear.

The hour when the sun would rise was drawing near. Maui crouched near the mouth of the cave, his eyes narrowed in focus for the first glimpse of the sun's light. Everything was ready, just as he had planned. His breath was steady, his head was clear, and his body was as taut as a bow before it releases an arrow.

A faint rumble reached his ears and he peered through the darkness. A weak beam of light flickered and faded. The sun was stirring. He made a sound with his tongue like an insect, signalling to his comrades to be alert. The rumble grew louder. Maui could see the dancing shadows on the walls of the cave lengthening and fading away as the light from the sun grew brighter. The cold of the morning was melting away in the heat, and Maui could feel sweat slowly beading his body. The sun was still way inside the cave, but his effects could be already be felt.

The first blinding ray of light to hit his eyes was the cue. Maui signalled to his people and they emerged from their hiding places, still camouflaged by the clay and vegetation. They took their positions, holding on to the braided flax ropes with all their strength. Maui was now so close to the sun that he felt like his flesh was on fire. He was burning up but he held strong. It would take just a few more moments.

As the sun emerged, rolling out at high speed, Maui shouted.

'NOW!'

He ran to the end of the flax rope that lay closest to him and began to pull. All the men and women followed his lead and pulled with all their strength. The ropes began to lift up from the ground.

The sun was caught completely unawares. Suddenly he found himself ensnared by thick flax ropes that began to tighten around him. He caught sight of Maui and roared furiously. Deep red angry flames shot out from him, singeing the ropes. The arms of the warriors grew slippery with perspiration as they gripped the ropes fiercely.

'Do not let go!' Maui shouted at the top of his voice. 'DO NOT LET GO!'

'What are you doing?' The sun yelled, burning with rage. 'Why are you trying to trap me? I will burn you all down.'

'DO NOT LET GO!' Maui shouted again, completely ignoring the sun.

The sun screamed in anger, throwing flames so high that the cave blazed with light, blinding the warriors. Still they held fast, muscles corded and bulging with tension; their feet sunk into the earth as if they had grown roots.

The ropes closed around the sun and snapped into place. He was now well and truly trapped. The more he struggled, the more the ropes tightened. Finally, he stopped struggling.

'What is the meaning of this?' He asked Maui. 'Do you know what you have done? By trapping me, you have stopped the cycle of life on earth. With no warmth and light, nothing will grow, and if nothing grows, life will end. Why have you trapped me thus?'

Maui stood akimbo, staring at the sun fearlessly.

'No doubt you are the giver of life, oh sun,' he said. 'But you have turned arrogant and unmindful of your duty. You race across the sky as if the demons from hell are chasing you. We can barely rise in the morning before it is already noon. And before we can complete our chores—do our hunting, gather our food and cook it—you have made your journey across the sky and are ready to sink beyond the horizon. We do not have time for anything. We are starving and dying because of you.'

The sun laughed.

'Is it my fault that you are so incompetent that you cannot complete your tasks in time? I am true to my nature. I hurtle across the sky at my pace, not at the pace you want me to.'

'You are not being true to your nature at all, oh sun,' Maui argued. 'You are hasty and impatient. You are supposed to be nurturing, yet you are not. Promise to slow down your pace, and I will set you free right away.'

'You are so foolish. You think, I, the mighty sun, will bow down to your stupid demand?'

'Very well then,' Maui said, rising to his full height. 'I have tried to be reasonable and to appeal to your better sense, but it appears you will not listen to reason or request. If force is the only way you will listen to me, so be it.'

'Force? You will force me?' The sun gave a mocking laugh. 'I'd like to see that.'

'So you shall,' Maui pronounced and produced the sacred jawbone from his belt.

The sun paled at the sight of it. This was no ordinary weapon, this could inflict the greatest pain.

'Let it be known that I gave the sun a fair chance,' Maui said to the men and women who had gathered around him, watching him in awe. 'He has refused to listen to our requests. I am left with no other option.'

With all his might, Maui raised the sacred jawbone and gave the sun a powerful blow. The sun screeched in agony. Again and again, Maui raised his weapon and rained blows on the sun. Finally, the sun succumbed, his pride broken.

'Stop, Maui, stop, I beg of you,' the sun cried. 'I will do as you have requested. I will not race across the skies. I will move at a slower pace so that you have enough time for your daily activities. I promise.'

'Do you promise by all that is sacred on this earth?' Maui asked, his arm still raised.

'Yes, yes, I promise. I swear I will abide by my oath. I will never go back on my word. I promise you.'

The group raised a loud cheer.

'You have all borne witness to the sun's promise,' Maui declared, lowering his arm and returning the sacred jawbone to his belt. 'Should we let him go now?'

The men and women agreed, and the ropes were all cut. The sun rose slowly into the sky, and his journey across the skies was as slow as the people needed. That day, they were able to do their hunting and gathering, cooking and eating at their desired pace. When at last the sun set on them, they danced around the fire and told their children how the great Maui had slowed the sun for them. And their children told their children and so on, and so the story reached us today. Isn't that just fantastic?

# Why the Crow Is Black

*Crows are really very clever birds. In Australian aboriginal culture, Crow is a hero She features in several interesting stories, including in one about bringing fire to humans. That is the story you will find below. Crow is not just a smart trickster, outwitting opponents, but she is also an old spirit carrying ancient knowledge, and is worthy of great respect.*

Crow was really hungry. She had hopped from branch to branch, had flown from tree to tree, had searched far and wide, but all she had managed to spot was yam. And she really hated yam.

'Ugh! Yuck!' She said, almost throwing up when she saw nothing but yam around. 'Will I never get anything else to eat in this dreadful place? I am going to die hungry for sure!'

She dramatically threw herself on the ground and lay very still, pretending to be dead. After a while she got tired and was about to pick herself up, when she heard the sound of footsteps. They didn't sound very close but they weren't very far either. She continued to lay still and kept her eyes closed, but every nerve of her body was on edge as she listened carefully.

'Here is a good spot,' she heard a woman say. 'It is nice and flat, perfect for preparing our dinner.'

'Yes, I agree,' said another woman. 'Let us set up

here for the night.'

There was quite a bit of noise and clatter as Crow listened closely. Carefully, she opened one eye and scanned her surroundings. She could see a group of women gathered together a few feet away. She counted: there were seven of them. Two of them were taking some yams out of their shawls; three of them were picking up twigs and sticks that were scattered around them; and two of them were setting up stones in a peculiar shape. They sang songs as they went about their tasks. When the stones were all set in the desired pattern, and the twigs and sticks were bundled into an opening in the pattern, the seven women stood around in a circle. They each held a staff in their hand, and the end of each staff glowed hot and red.

Was that burning coal?

Crow could hardly believe her eyes as they danced to a slow rhythm around the stones, their voices joined in a strange chant. Every now and then they pounded their staffs into the ground. When the chant was over, they held the glowing ends of the staffs over the twigs. To Crow's astonishment, a flame jumped between the twigs and soon the women had a fire going.

One of the women placed a few yams on the stones, and as they continued their singing and telling of stories, she turned the yams over every few minutes. Soon a delicious aroma filled the air. Crow's stomach began to rumble with hunger. Oh! If only she could taste just a morsel! Her mouth was watering.

When the yams were cooked to their satisfaction, the fire was put out and the women sat around, chatting in low voices and eating their dinner. The sun hung low over the horizon, and the shadows lengthened as the day melted into night. Crow lay as still as a corpse, for she dared not rise and bring attention to herself. Soon darkness shrouded the land, and the murmurs of the women faded as they drifted off to sleep.

Finally, when Crow was certain that she would not be spotted, she rose and moved quietly to where the fire had been. She was so hungry that she would gladly have eaten the raw yams right then and there! As luck would have it, a piece of cooked yam lay behind the fireplace. Most likely it had been dropped by one of the women and had gone unnoticed. Crow wasted no time and began eating the cooked yam. Her eyes grew wide at the first taste. It was beyond delicious—it was divinely scrumptious! Suddenly, she froze. One of the young ladies had woken up and was looking right at her! Would she sound the alarm? Would she shoo Crow away?

Instead, the young lady just smiled, shook her head, and went back to sleep.

Crow heaved a sigh of relief. That was a close call! But the yam was too delectable and worth the risk. Before she knew it, she had gobbled up all of it.

'That's it!' Crow decided. 'I am never going to eat raw yam again in my entire life. Cooked yam is it for me.'

But she soon realized that she had a bigger problem. Without fire, she would not be able to cook her yams. And she could get fire only from the glowing coals. Would she be able to persuade the women to give her one of their coals? Would they be willing? Well, she would give it a try and ask them as soon as the sun rose, she thought. The cooked yams were too delicious to give up. She had never ever tasted anything so yummy in her entire life, and there was no way she was going away without a piece of glowing coal!

Crow hopped onto a tree and dozed off. There were only a few more hours before daybreak, and she wanted to make sure that she was in good shape to meet the women and make her request.

In the blink of an eye, or so it seemed, tendrils of weak sunlight began to creep into the sky and the dark night lightened as the sun rose. Crow immediately sat up straight and looked across to where the women lay asleep. They were still in deep slumber, so she flew over to a nearby rivulet and freshened herself. She groomed herself so that she looked neat and tidy and not a feather was out of place. When she returned, the women had awoken and were talking to each other in low voices. They were rolling up their shawls and gathering their belongings.

Crow surveyed the women carefully. Whom could she approach? She would have preferred the young lady who had been so kind to her last night, but it was clear that it was the oldest woman who was the leader.

Crow was sick with anxiety, but she knew it was now or never. She tapped her beak against the branch and flew down as elegantly as she could. She perched on a stone outcrop and cleared her throat with a loud caw. The women stopped what they were doing and looked at her in surprise.

'Dear ladies,' she said, bowing low before the leader. 'I hope you will give me a few minutes of your precious time. I have a request to make. Do I have your permission to proceed?'

The women glanced at each other, trying to suppress their laughter. How pompous Crow sounded! The oldest woman nodded her head and waved a hand for Crow to proceed.

'Thank you. Good morning. I am Crow and I have come to you with a request. I have been eating raw yam ever since I was born and I am quite sick of it. I had a taste of your cooked yam last night, and I liked it very much indeed. So much so that I have vowed to eat only cooked yam for the rest of my life. But I need fire to cook the yam, and you have the fire at the end of your staffs. I would really like it very much if you could give me one of your burning coals, so that I can also make a fire and cook my yam. Then I can forever eat cooked yam to my heart's content.'

The astonishment on the women's faces at such a strange request was obvious. Two of them rolled their eyes, two of them slapped their foreheads with their hands, and three of them shook their heads, grimacing.

The leader spoke softly.

'Crow, did I hear you right? You stole our food last night and today you want us to give you fire?'

'Well,' Crow defended herself, 'it isn't technically stealing if I eat a piece of dropped food, is it? And since you are the only ones with fire, who else could I ask?'

The women all gathered in a circle and began discussing in low voices. Crow strained to hear what they were saying, but they were speaking too softly for her to hear anything. She didn't understand why they were creating such a scene. Surely, it wasn't as if they couldn't spare her a piece of the burning coal!

She grew annoyed and finally asked in a loud impatient tone, 'Is there a problem? Or can I get my piece of burning coal and get going? I am rather hungry, you know. So why don't you hurry up?'

The group broke up and the oldest woman stepped forward.

'Well, Crow,' she replied, 'it is rather presumptuous of you to imagine we will just hand over a piece of burning coal, just so that you can eat cooked yam for the rest of your life. Fire is sacred and for that reason, there are only seven burning coals in the whole world. I am sorry, but we will not be giving you anything. You have been rude and haughty with us, and I hope you will learn to be a bit more polite and humble. You may leave us now.'

Crow's opened her beak, but she could hardly speak. She was rude? Well, what were these women then? They were even ruder and haughtier than she was! Who did they think they were? She would get her fire with or without their help.

Without a word, she flapped her wings and flew away as fast as she could. She would teach these women a lesson. She would get the burning coal she deserved, and these women would then learn not to be so dismissive. Polite and humble indeed. Bah!

Crow sat deep in thought on a branch of the tallest tree. She would have to come up with a really innovative plan to get the coal from the women. How would she do that?

The sun was at the highest point in the sky and was blazing down on the land below. Just when Crow was about to give up in despair, she spied something below her. A light bulb went off in her head. Oh, this was perfect! She was beside herself with glee and gave herself a nice pat on the back. Clever Crow, she told herself, you are the smartest bird in the entire land for sure!

Crow waited as the sun descended in the western sky. A gentle and cool evening breeze blew and birds called to each other as they began to fly back to their nests. Little four-legged creatures were scurrying back to their burrows and tree holes. Crow could see the seven women approaching. She took a look at herself once again—she looked just like she wanted to: smart, with neat feathers and a shiny beak.

As the women walked beneath her tree, she flew down slowly, flapping her wings in a rather shaky way.

'Look who's come to visit us again,' said the first woman, with a smirk on her face, as Crow landed near her.

'I hope you're not going to beg for coal again!' said the second woman, rolling her eyes.

'Still hungry for cooked yam?' The young woman from the previous night asked with a kind smile.

'Actually...', Crow paused dramatically, then strutted a bit and turned to them, '...no!'

*'What?'* The women halted in astonishment, hardly able to believe their ears. 'You're not following us around to ask us to share our cooked yam or our burning coal?'

Crow laughed.

'You know,' she said thoughtfully. 'I have a surprise for you. I had a good mind not to share this with you after this morning's events, when you accused me of being rude and proud. But I wanted to prove to you that I am neither rude nor proud, so I have decided to share this very good news with you. I am sure you will really appreciate it and thank me later.'

'Really?' The women eyed her in disbelief. 'What is the surprise that you so kindly want to share with us?

Go ahead, we are waiting with bated breath.'

'Well,' Crow began, 'after I tasted your cooked yam, I was convinced that there was nothing else on earth that could be more delicious. I thought I had died and gone to heaven when I ate that piece of cooked yam. But you know what? Within the space of a few hours, cooked yam was completely knocked off from the top of the list. I was of course taken aback. I could not believe that I was lucky enough to get to taste not just one, but *two* delicious dishes in one day—each more yummy than anything I had eaten before. But life can be strange indeed. It gave me two treats today!'

'Oh, is that right?' The women scoffed. 'Tell us, Crow, what is this super scrumptious dish that you claim is better than cooked yam?'

Crow flew up to a low-hanging branch, which just high enough to be out of reach of the women.

'I will not just tell you,' she said graciously, 'I will also show you where you can get it.'

'I'm hungry,' said the first woman, rubbing her stomach. 'Hurry up, Crow, and tell us where this delicious food is.

Crow pointed with her wing to an anthill that was a little further away from where they were standing.

'There it is,' she said with a flourish.

'Where? Where?' The women peered into the distance, some of them shading their eyes with their hands. 'All we see is an anthill.'

'Precisely,' replied Crow. 'The ant larvae that you will find in that anthill are to die for! So mouth-wateringly delicious! You will never want to eat your cooked yam again. Bleh!' She said, making a gagging gesture.

'Ant larvae?' The women looked at each other. 'Really?

'Trust me,' said Crow, looking very serious and dropping her voice into a whisper. 'I am sharing this information with you only out of sheer gratitude for the piece of cooked yam you gave me yesterday. No one else knows, cross my heart.'

'I'd really like to try some ant larvae,' said one of the women eagerly. 'I am quite sick of cooked yam, aren't you?'

The others agreed. 'Let's go get some ant larvae!

As they set off towards the anthill, Crow flew higher and made sure to hide herself very well in the tree. This way she would have a clear view of the women without being seen herself. The women approached the anthill and began digging into it.

The anthill was actually an abandoned one; it had now been taken over by a large family of snakes. The snakes had been settling in for the night when all of a sudden they heard pounding on the ground above them, and the walls of the anthill began to crumble. Furious at the invasion, the snakes swarmed out of the anthill, ready to attack the culprits.

When the women saw the snakes emerging from the anthill, they panicked. They began hitting the snakes with their staffs violently. In the ensuing melee, some of the coals flew off the staffs and landed a few feet away. This was exactly what Crow had been waiting for.

She flew down swiftly, picked up the burning coals, and shoved them into a bag made of kangaroo skin. When the bag was almost full, she tried to fly away. But the bag was too heavy. She would not be able to take off with it.

The noise made by the women had attracted all the birds and animals. Some of them noticed what Crow was up to.

'There she is,' one of them yelled. 'She's stealing the coals from the women.'

They crowded behind her as she finally managed to take off. She flew up to a higher branch, but the animals and birds had her surrounded.

'Throw us some coals too,' they yelled. 'Throw us some of the burning coals too.'

'Why don't I cook something for you all?' Crow said, trying to distract them. 'I can cook a really delicious dinner for us all.'

But the mob was not willing to relent. In fact, to Crow's dismay, some of the creatures began to climb the tree, or flew up to perch near her. She began to back away, clutching the bag of coals.

'Give it to us! Give it to us!' their chant grew louder. Crow's terror also grew. As they closed in around her, she shrieked in horror and flung the burning coals away. Unfortunately for her, the day had been dry and hot, and the dry brush and twigs caught fire immediately.

'The land is on fire! The land is on fire!' The screams and cries of all the fleeing creatures filled the air. The branch on which Crow was sitting also caught fire and flames engulfed her. She began flapping her wings furiously and managed to put the fire out. But, by then, her body had been burnt black.

Crow's trick unfortunately backfired. And that is why, apparently, crows are black to this day.

# Anansi Wins the Stories

*Anansi is a well-known figure in African and Caribbean cultures. He is known to assume the form of a spider (perhaps the very first Spiderman, or even Spidergod!). He is great at coming up with creative solutions to knotty problems and outsmarting others with his cunning wit, and so his name is also synonymous with wisdom. His stories have been handed down orally from one generation to another. In this one, we see how he becomes the God of all stories through his quick thinking.*

When the world began, there were no stories. Nyame, the Sky-God, hoarded all the stories of the world and whenever anyone asked for a tale, he would demand a price that was so high that no one could afford it. The price could be anything—an impossibly large fortune or the nectar of the Gods. Whatever it was, it was always beyond anyone's reach. And thus it was that people all across Africa lived in sorrow and without entertainment, for who does not like a good story? Finally, they approached Anansi, the Spider. If there was anyone who could buy the stories from Nyame, it had to be Anansi, who was renowned for his intelligence, wisdom, and ability to outwit anyone. He would surely come up with a way to free the stories from the unreasonable Sky-God.

Anansi thought for a moment, then agreed. It would indeed be good to have all the stories to share.

He went to Nyame immediately.

'I'd like to buy all your stories, Nyame,' he said, after they had greeted each other.

Nyame looked at him with surprise.

'Are you sure, Anansi? Would you really like to buy *all* my stories? You know the price is really, really high, don't you? Why, so many people before you have tried. They were from wealthier families and from more powerful kingdoms. And even though they tried with all their might, they failed miserably. They have all given up and gone away. Are you sure you want to try?'

Anansi shrugged. 'Tell me the price, Nyame. Only then I can determine whether I can afford it or not, right? If I can't afford it, then no harm done. But if I can, then it's a win-win: you get your rightful price and I get the stories. What do you have to lose?'

Nyame stared at Anansi with narrowed eyes. Could he trust this strange-looking human-spider hybrid with eight legs and an innocent grin on his face? Was the spider trying to trick him somehow? But Anansi did seem sincere this time.

'All right,' Nyame finally conceded after a long moment. 'I'll tell you the price and you tell me if you can afford it, OK? There are three things you must bring me.'

Anansi nodded. 'And they are?' He asked.

'First, you must bring me Mmoboro, the Hornets. You must have heard how painful their stings are, right? It is almost impossible to trap them, let alone bringing them anywhere. Second, you must bring me Onini, the great python. He will squeeze you to a painful death if you are not careful, you understand? Lastly, I must have Osebo, the leopard. He is so fast that he can jump on you and tear you into little pieces in the blink of an eye.'

'That's it? Mmoboro, Onini, and Osebo? If I bring them to you, you will give me all the stories?' Anansi asked with a deadpan face.

Nyame laughed. 'I like your confidence, Anansi! Yes, you bring these three to me, and I will hand all my stories over to you along with my blessings.'

'Very well then, you have a deal,' Anansi smiled.

Nyame shook his head as Anansi walked away with a swagger. Nyame chortled. Did the spider really think he would be successful?

Anansi went home and had a long discussion with his wife Aso. They came up with various strategies and plans and finally agreed on the way forward.

The next morning, Anansi went to his garden and selected a nice, big gourd. He used a sharpened twig to make a small hole in it. Then he rolled some grass into a taut bundle so that it served to plug the hole completely. Once he had tested the contraption, he picked up a vessel and filled it with water. All set, he packed the gourd with the hole, the grass plug, and the vessel filled with water and then made his way to the tree where the Mmoboro hornets lived.

The hornets were busy buzzing about and did not notice Anansi arriving at their tree. They looked large and dangerous. They had yellow markings on their blackish-brown bodies and they were flying about aggressively. At the right moment, when the hornets were really busy, Anansi threw some of the water from the vessel on himself so that he was drenched and dripping. He quickly threw the rest of the water on the hornets, so that they too got drenched. Then he upturned the vessel on his head, as if protecting himself.

'Oh dear! Oh dear! How heavily it is raining! I am already so wet, I will get drenched in no time,' he said loudly. Then, as if noticing the wet hornets for the first time, he called out to them.

'Hey! Why are you all out in the rain? It is going to start raining even more heavily. You will get so wet you won't be able to fly. You might even get washed away! Aren't you worried?'

'Of course we are worried!' buzzed the hornets. 'But where do we go? We need a dry place.' The foolish hornets had not bothered to look up at the skies to see whether it was really raining.

'Oh, silly me!' Anansi slapped his forehead and picked up the gourd in which he had made the hole. 'I have just the right place for you. Get inside this gourd at once, and you can remain nice and dry, away from this rain.'

'How do we get in?' buzzed the anxious hornets, crowding around the gourd. 'How do we get in?'

'I think there's a hole somewhere here...wait...here it is!' Anansi pretended to search for the hole. 'Hurry, get in before the downpour gets heavier!'

The hornets all rushed into the gourd through the hole. Anansi waited till the last one was in. Then he neatly plugged the hole with the grass bundle.

'Did they seriously fall for my little ruse?' He shook his head in wonder and said, 'Well, that's one of the three things Nyame wanted. Let me get this to him as soon as I can. I don't want to wait and see what the angry hornets will do once they realize they've been tricked and traded.'

Nyame could hardly contain his surprise when Anansi handed him the gourd.

'Here you go,' he said, 'here's the first condition met—the Mmoboro. All safely captured in the gourd.'

Nyame was impressed despite himself. He had to admit that this was some quick and smart thinking by Anansi.

'What about the other two?' he couldn't help asking.

'Working on it. Don't worry, you'll get them soon enough.' Anansi grinned.

That afternoon, Anansi walked into the forest carrying a bamboo pole and some vines. The forest was thick with vegetation and it was dark, with the trees closing in overhead and barely letting any sunlight through. He was muttering to himself, loud enough for anyone interested to overhear what he was saying. Of course, Anansi had planned all this in order to capture Onini, the menacing python. He walked in the direction of the python's usual resting place. It was always coiled on the branch of the biggest tree in the middle of the forest.

Onini was sunning himself when he heard Anansi's loud muttering. He listened carefully and got more and more puzzled by what he heard.

'She is a silly woman, my wife, that's for sure. What does she know? I roam in the jungle, and I know what I'm talking about. And if I say that he is as long and as strong, she should believe me and accept it as fact. But does she? No! Instead, she argues with me, the foolish woman! She says he is much shorter and much weaker. She cannot believe that I give him so much respect. He doesn't deserve it, she says. Well, she's wrong!' Anansi kept muttering to himself in this manner for a few minutes.

Onini could not contain his curiosity and finally emerged from under the grass.

'Anansi!' he called out, slithering his way to the spider. 'What are you debating so hard with yourself? Who is arguing with you and giving you such a hard time?'

Anansi shook his head and sighed, a woeful look on his face. He placed the bamboo pole and the vines on the ground, stretched out his eight tired limbs and sat down on his haunches.

'It's my wife,' he said mournfully. 'I am so tired of arguing with her from morning to night. She never accepts anything I say. Even if I state a fact like the sun shines during the day, she will argue with me, I am sure.' He let out a deep sigh.

Onini made a sympathetic noise, not sure what to say.

'Take today,' Anansi continued grumbling. 'Can you believe it? The woman has the audacity to say that you are shorter and weaker than this bamboo pole? I tell her: Wife, listen to me. I have seen Onini with my own two eyes. I swear upon my life that he is longer than this bamboo pole, and there is absolutely no question that he is stronger than it. But does she listen? No! The infuriating woman insists that she is right. How do I make her realize she is wrong? She is so wrong!'

'Now, now,' Onini said in a calming voice. 'There's no need to get all worked up. You know what? I know the perfect solution. Here I am. And here is the bamboo pole. Let us measure me against it. You will have your proof!'

'Oh Onini! You are so smart!' Anansi brightened. 'Yes, let us do just that. Come, lie down next to the pole. Put your head right at the top of the pole. Here... perfect! Now let me go to the other end and measure you against the pole.'

Onini lay perfectly still and stretched himself beside the pole.

'Such a silly fellow this Anansi is,' he thought to himself. 'Thanks to my smart thinking, at least he can now prove to his wife that his answer is correct.'

'Onini!' Anansi called, from where he was positioned at the tail. 'You seem to be slightly shorter than the pole. Are you stretching yourself all the way?'

'I am,' Onini answered, as he stretched himself some more. 'How is it looking now?'

'You need to stretch a little more,' Anansi called out in reply. 'Just a little. Ah, there!'

He came back to the head of the pole and frowned.

'What happened?' Onini asked.

'It looks like when you stretched, your head slipped and came a little lower down the pole. We'll have to measure you again. I have an idea. Let me use these vines and tie your head to the pole. That way you won't slip lower when you stretch.'

'Good idea!' Onini agreed. He waited till Anansi finished tying him up with the vines. But Anansi didn't stop with his head. He went on binding the vines tightly all the way down, till the python could barely move.

'What are you doing?' Onini hissed in anger, as he tried to break free. 'Why have you tied me up so tightly?'

Anansi grinned at him. 'Looks like my wife is a smart woman after all,' he winked. 'You are certainly shorter than this bamboo pole, and definitely weaker, since you aren't able to break free!'

'You tricked me!' Onini hissed again.

'Yes. I did,' Anansi nodded. 'I'm sorry, but this is the only payment Nyame is ready to accept. It's not my fault that you fell for my unbelievable story.'

Hefting the bamboo pole with the bound python

onto his shoulder, Anansi made his way to the Sky-God.

'Back already?' Nyame asked, raising an eyebrow.

'Well, here's your second condition met,' Anansi said, laying the pole—with Onini tied to it—at Nyame's feet.

'This is...astonishing!' Nyame spluttered, his mouth agape in wonder as he saw the fat python that was valiantly trying to break free from the vine.

'Thank you very much!' Anansi bowed with a smirk. 'Well, the last present will also be brought to you soon, so I hope you are ready to hand over all your stories.'

He turned and walked away, leaving an astounded Nyame in his wake. The Sky-God had definitely underestimated Anansi's abilities. And soon, he would have to pay for it.

Anansi did not waste any time. He immediately started getting prepared to snare Osebo, the leopard. He knew exactly where the leopard liked to roam, so he carefully laid a trap in the area. He dug a deep hole, then covered it with mud and leaves so that it looked like the ground was undisturbed. All that work left him tired. So he rested on the bough of a tree, waiting for his efforts to yield fruit, as an inky dusk rapidly enveloped the forest.

Soon enough, he heard a rustle in the undergrowth, and then a crash and an unmistakable yowl.

'It had worked!' Anansi pumped all eight fists in victory. He settled down for a peaceful night, knowing that in the morning, he would have to deal with a very irate leopard indeed.

The next day, Anansi clambered down the tree and peered over the edge of the pit. He could see Osebo pacing impatiently. The magnificent beast with its beautiful spotted skin, flicking its white-tipped tail in irritation, was a sight to behold.

'Hello there!' He called. 'Why are you down there in a pit?'

'I'm not down here by choice, you imbecile!' Osebo snapped in anger. 'I've fallen into a trap, can't you see? Or are you blind as well as stupid?'

'Oh,' Anansi replied, scratching his head. 'You've fallen into a trap? How are you going to get out?'

Osebo paused for a moment, then adjusted his tone to a more placatory one.

'My friend, seeing as you are the only one who knows about my predicament, how about you help me, eh? Just put your hand out, and I can haul myself up. I can tell that you are a helpful sort, aren't you? Do me a favour and get some blessings in return. I'll owe you big-time.'

'Ha!' Anansi said scornfully. 'I may be stupid but I am not *that* stupid, you know. I have a family. I have a wife and kids who are waiting for me. Let's say out of the kindness of my heart, I actually pull you out. Then what? You are going to pounce on me and rip me into tasty little bits for your lunch, aren't you? I'm not going to be taken in by your sweet words. I don't want to do you any favours or have you owe me any favours either. I'm leaving right now.'

Anansi disappeared from the edge, and Osebo called out to him in an urgent, pleading tone.

'Wait, please! Please wait! Don't leave me. I swear to you I will not eat you up. I won't even so much as scratch you, I promise! Please, please help me out of this terrible trap, I beg you.'

After a moment, Anansi appeared again.

'How do I know you will keep your word?' he called out. 'How do I believe you?'

'What do you want me to do?' Osebo replied, frustrated and desperate. 'Tell me, I'll do whatever you want.'

Anansi thought for a little bit.

'OK, I have an idea. But you must do exactly as I say, all right? Otherwise, I will just leave.'

'Sure,' promised Osebo. 'I'll do exactly as you say.'

Anansi went over to a tall tree that stood at the edge of the pit. He tied a rope to the top of the tree, and began pulling it down, so that it began to form an arch over the pit. When the top was close to the mouth of the pit, he tied the rope down to another tree trunk, so that it remained in that position.

He then tied another rope to the top of the tree and threw its other end into the pit.

'Do you see the rope I just threw down?' Anansi called out to Osebo.

'Yes, I see it. What do you want me to do with it?'

'Tie it to your tail. Tie it really tightly so that you don't break loose. If you do, you could fall down and break your neck and die.'

'All right,' Osebo agreed, suppressing a shudder that ran through his body. He didn't want to die in the pit, but he definitely also didn't want to fall and die. So he tied the rope really tightly to his tail and tugged at it to make sure it was holding firm.

'You done?' Anansi called again.

'Yes, my tail is tightly bound, no chance of getting loose,' Osebo replied. 'What now?'

'Hang on, and I mean that literally!' Anansi laughed and said. Then, with a quick swipe, he cut the first rope that had held the tree in position over the pit. The tree snapped back to an upright position, with Osebo hanging on for dear life, as he dangled from the very top of the tree by his tail.

'Oh dear! Oh dear!' Osebo closed his eyes, sick with fear as the tree swayed vigorously to and fro, throwing him this way and that, shaking him like a leaf in a storm. He felt nauseous and faint, and as he caught sight of the ground below him—which seemed a very far way away—he blacked out completely.

'Now who's the stupid one?' Anansi said softly under his breath as he cut the leopard down.

Nyame woke up to the sight of a passed-out leopard slung across Anansi's shoulders.

'Good morning, Nyame!' Anansi said cheerfully, as he swung the unconscious leopard into a heap at the Sky-God's feet. 'There, I've met the third condition, as promised!'

'Good heavens, Anansi!' Nyame exclaimed, jumping to his feet. 'I cannot believe it! You have outdone yourself. I could not have chosen a more worthy person myself. You are smart and brave, and you are the perfect fit to be the inheritor of all the stories of the world. Good work!'

And thus, as the setting sun painted the sky gold and purple, all the beasts and all the people gathered around, cheering and applauding as Nyame handed over all the stories to Anansi. A great celebration was organized, and there was much dancing, singing, and feasting to honour Anansi, who had become the owner of the treasure-trove of beautiful stories from around the world—this one included!

So, if you ever narrate this story to anyone else, don't forget to mention that it is Anansi's tale.